Highwire

Act

*& other tales
of survival*

HIGHWIRE ACT

& other tales of survival

JoeAnn Hart

BLACK LAWRENCE PRESS

www.blacklawrence.com

Executive Editor: Diane Goettel

Cover and interior design: Zoe Norvell
Cover Artwork: "Catch and Released" by Hans Pundt

Copyright ©JoeAnn Hart 2023
ISBN: 978-1-62557-058-1

Published 2023 by Black Lawrence Press.
Printed in the United States.

TO ANNIE, JACK, AND ELLE,
THE FUTURE OF THE WORLD.

Table of Contents

Reef of Plagues

THESE TOURISTS ARE nothing but trouble, slapping and grinding through the water in their power cruisers, searching for a place to snorkel. Better luck milking a fish, we tell them and they give us the rough side of their tongues. It was not so long ago we were adjusting their masks, leading them to where sapphire light once shone through branched cathedrals, the coral luminous as jewels. Our precious riches. Don't touch, we say, again and again, this is not a treasure hunt. The reef is still the source of our living for those of us who are left, those who survived the first few seasons of sinking tourism. Who wants to visit a Hades of bleached bones?

"Hey!" a bright-pink man shouts from a vessel that has snuck up on us. "Hey!"

We look at one another to see who's game. Our broad backs are to the sun, men and women alike, our bellies to the rubber boats as we scoop water samples into vials, scrape slime from lifeless coral, and take the reef's temperature as we would a dear child's. Out in deep water, buoys do all this and more, sending messages through the clear air to the office computers. But the sensors can only monitor, not mourn it as we do. For years now, the coral has been fading like a shadow on the water, but no help came until the tourists themselves became endangered. The scientists do not discuss what will happen if the reef dies altogether, but we can read the signs. We know our fate.

The pink man believes the problem is that we cannot hear him so he inches closer, one eye keen on his depth finder. Electronics are not magic; it insults the gods to navigate a vessel like that in shallow water. Even we in our inflatable dinghies cannot always use our outboards and must pull with our oars. But that is not our job to tell him. Not anymore.

The man tests his luck and gets quite close. The cruiser begins panting in neutral, then suddenly he is on his deck waving at us. "Excuse me! Over here!"

We groan. We are sick of explaining the obvious to the oblivious. It is too damn hot. "What?" one of us answers. We know, of course, what he wants, but we pretend innocence. We lean back and drink deeply of our canteens as we look up at him.

"What happened to this place?" the man asks. He takes off his baseball cap and sunglasses and wipes his boneless face with his loud shirt. He is wide and top-heavy, like his black-hulled boat, which flies an American flag. His red hair is almost plucked clean, so with his sunburnt skin he looks like a tufted bloodworm. His two pastel children, slick with sunscreen—and we hope it is not the slop that poisons the reef—stare at us. A pale woman, the man's wife, we guess, looks down into her wineglass, searching. An old man, a crumpled version of the pink man, lies on a lounge chair with closed eyes and an open book.

Do we pretend to more innocence? We do.

"Happened? What do you mean, happened?" another one of us asks. We no longer have to be nice to tourists, so we're not. Besides, the sick reef is their fault. That is what our bosses hint at. They say our coral is dying because the world burns too much oil, and it is sure as hell not us doing the burning. Every day, we must scrounge gas for our scooters to get us to the dock.

The man presses his great stomach against the rail, and as he leans forward to talk to us his skin flushes. Like the seaworm, he should not be out in the sun. "We've been going around in circles. Where's the coral? The fish? I told my kids it would be like swimming in a high-end aquarium."

We all look at one another as if we haven't a clue. One of us peers into the water, then sits bolt upright and shouts "Great Zeus, the reef is dead!" We all look horrified into the sea as if we don't know shit.

The man cannot tell if we are pulling his tender leg.

"I give up," the woman says. On stormy days we hang around

the office and our bosses show videos from cameras miles below the surface. We marvel at the strange greenish-white creatures at the very bottom of the sea. That is the color of this woman's skin. "I told you we should have gone to Atlantis instead," she says to the horizon.

"These kids need to experience real nature, not a water park," he tells her. "I don't want them to grow up sheltered from the world." He pauses as if considering. "Like you."

We shake our heads. You cannot speak to your woman like that or there will be a price to pay. He has a sickly smile on his face as she whispers something to him we cannot quite hear over the hissing of the surf, either "Fuck you" or "I'm warning you." She finishes her glass of wine, turns to the cabin and disappears into the cavernous space. The children pay no mind to either of them. They have blue flippers on their feet and snorkeling masks in their little hands, ready to receive the world's blessings. We look past them, squinting into the strong sun to watch a pelican drop headlong like Icarus into the sea. We wait for him to rise in glory, a feasting bird, but he comes up with an empty beak. Even the charter boats must go far out to sea now while our people hold empty nets on the shore.

"What have you done to the coral?" the man asks, pointing at our equipment. "The last time I was here it was a tropical wonderland."

We? We stare at him blankly and some of us go back to work. We have to get ourselves to Half Moon Bay where our bosses think they saw signs of black band disease in a healthy colony. They want us to suit up and dive with them for coral samples. Time is not on our side.

"I want to see the fishes, Daddy," says the little girl.

"I want to see a shipwreck," says the boy.

Ah, so would we, on both accounts. Rusted hulks used to sit where they landed on the reef, left as a warning to other mariners. We would collect some fine things from those boats. Our homes are made with so much salvage that the priests joke that we live in salvation. But now the tourist board, grown nervous and defensive, tows the vessels out to sea before we can get to them. They say tourists do not want to see that nature's power is greater than their own.

"You must have been here a long time ago," one of us says. "This part of the reef has been dead or dying for a good eight years."

"What do you mean dead?" the man asks. "Have you ever seen coral? It's just a rock. A colorful rock."

It is alive, or was, we tell him. Tiny animals, polyps. They grow a shell, creating hard and beautiful homes, and live on algae. We do not waste breath explaining symbiosis to this man, but tell him how the algae determines the color of coral, which grows in many shapes. We know them all by name. Elliptical Star, Boulder Brain, Corky Sea Finger, Mustard Hill, Yellow Pencil. We learned the language of sea life when we were guides; now we must learn the language of sea death. Not just bleaching, but disease. Yellow Band,

White Band, Black Band. White Plague, White Pox. The reef is so sick it can no longer give birth to the tiny organisms from which spring the great chains of being. Now, clear jellyfish float like dead spirits through a labyrinth of thighbones and skulls. "Warmer water stresses the polyps and they eject the algae," we say. "That is the bleaching that makes them look like skeletons. Sometimes they heal themselves, but lately, no. They die in a shroud of slime."

"Polyps?" the man says. "I know all about those. I had four polyps removed from my colon last year. Benign, totally benign. I had two removed a few years before that. If I can grow new polyps, so can this reef."

We wonder if he is now pulling our legs. There is no way of knowing. Their brains are as dense as conch meat. We pause at our labors and inhale the salty breath of the ocean.

"We wish we could help you," one of us finally says, although we do not wish that at all. "We have work to do. Parts of the reef on the other side of the island are still alive. Go there."

"I don't have time to motor all the way around the island," the man explains, as if we simply misunderstand his problem. "We're on a tight schedule. Today's the day for snorkeling."

Music comes blaring from the cabin. It is the woman's way of getting her man's attention, or it is her way of drowning him out. "ABBA!" we exclaim. "Cassandra." A song that is no "Dancing Queen," but sounds good to our ears. We hum the refrain and continue our work. The man goes to shout into the cabin and we forget about him altogether when we find a sea turtle tangled in plastic filament. We pull him close with a grapple and cut the fishing gear away. But it is too late. Too late even to eat him and give his death meaning. It never ends. Last week we found a bloated manatee in a ghost net, his soft whiskered face nibbled away by the fishes.

The man returns. The music has stopped.

"Taking those water samples isn't going to help anything, if you don't mind me saying so." The man says this with such a smile, we can tell he's figured out how to fix our problem. "You should be spending your time building the coral back up. We visitors spend a lot money here, you can afford to bring in new polyps. Get some biotech company to engineer ones that can tolerate warmer water." He grips the railing tight with satisfaction. We look at one another. Create a new species? We hadn't thought of that. Maybe that's because we are not gods.

Speaking of the divine. The cabin door opens and out comes not his wife but a semi-goddess at one with the elements. She walks on deck as if she'd rather fly, but keeps her ravishing feet on earth as a courtesy to us lesser beings. Before she puts on her sunglasses, she pauses to stare at us with her wide-set eyes, gray as deep water.

"It's out of our hands," one of us says to the man. "We can't bring back the dead."

The children have abandoned their masks and flippers and are eating some sort of sticky ambrosia that the young woman, who must be their babysitter and not a goddess after all, is bestowing on them. She looks at us as if she would like to share the bounty, but we are too far away for her beneficence.

One of us starts rolling up some herb. We can't seem to let him alone.

"What are you doing?" he asks, rising to the bait. "You can't do that here."

We light up the spliff and hand it around, leaning from one raft to another. The man gathers his children before they can smell the sweet smoke and pushes them into the cabin. The babysitter looks at us with longing.

"It's just Mother Nature," we explain to the man, smiling.

"It's a drug," he says. "And I won't have it around my family. I think it might be time to leave this island."

Some of us, whose hands are not busy with work or weed, applaud. This makes pink man purple. His throat is like a dark mast and we wonder if he might burst. The babysitter steps towards him, and even though she says nothing, he takes a breath. Then another. "The hell with this pimple of Caribbean dirt," he says calmly, pulling his dignity around him. He turns away just as the wind shifts a bit. The boat adjusts, making him unsteady on his feet, and he trips on the lounge where the old man lies. The book slips to the deck. The old man does not wake and we wonder if he is even alive. When the babysitter bends down for the book, pink man, still trying to get his balance, bumps into her, knocking off her sunglasses. We feel the crack right through our hearts. "Sorry," he says to her then retreats up to the helm, muttering. She picks up her glasses and squints at him through the empty frame in a way that makes us shiver.

Rosy-gray cumuli appear on the water's horizon as the man puts his cruiser in gear. We are losing time, but we wait to see if our curs'd mariner can turn his boat around in such shallow waters. Sweat bleeds from his pores, but he does it. We have to give him credit. His stern faces us. *Odyssey*, Annapolis, Maryland.

"This man is very far from home," we say.

As the boat motors off, it leaves fingers of dark oil on the water. We watch him head out the wrong channel, but we find that our tongues lie heavy in our mouths. His depth finder will not tell him he is in trouble until it is too late, and soon enough, he doesn't have enough water to piss in. We hear the lifeless reef scrape his bottom and hold him tight. We go back to work. We are very busy collecting samples. By the time he bucks his vessel back and forth to free himself, there is a small puncture in his hull. Good luck with that, we say to ourselves. Good bloody luck. He leaves in a cloud of reeking fumes and we hear him curse the heavens. He is a man of poor judgment but more creative with his words than we would have guessed.

"How far do you think he'll get?" we ask one another.

"Too far for us to help. Much too far."

We watch the babysitter, regal in her beauty, standing like a statue on the transom of the cruiser. As the man struggles to navigate towards open water, she unties her tunic from behind her neck and pulls it over her head. She stands before the reef like an Aphrodite in a silvery bathing suit, born on the half shell. She is slim-legged and smooth as a smelt. A thin gold belt embraces her waist like a wedding ring. She places her palms together and touches the tips of her fingers to her rosy lips, then raises her arms and dives like a marlin to windward, displacing a perfect arc of water that captures the sunlight. Drops splash on the old man and he sits up, blinking. Her body moves swiftly through the turquoise temple of water, gliding just beneath the surface. Her hair floats, then submerges, as she goes deeper, dissolving into the sea like salt. The old man stands with difficulty and raises a palsied hand. The wind stirs the water so that she is no longer visible, but we know she is there because small ecstatic fish leap at her approach. Love water, we hear them sing. Love the water! Our hearts are high with excitement. Daughter of the mighty sea, she's come to save us, or she's come to destroy us. Either way, we hold our breath and wait to see her rise.

Highwire Act

THE LILTING VOICE that fell like water from the loudspeaker every morning predicted an almost perfect day. "A sky as blue as my right eye," she called it. They have a way of letting us see the world through the odd detail. No matter. It's a blue sky and I'm an industrious soul, so my thoughts turned to laundry. I'd done the wash days before when it first started to rain then waited for a dry spell to hang it. And waited. The dome was supposed to be weather resistant but the drains are always clogged so the weather has nowhere to go but through the wonky seams, and if untreated water touches my clothes, well then, I'll be in worse shape than when I started. The laundry was beginning to smell like a mushroom log but a few hours in the open rotunda would soon cure that.

I grabbed my basket and slid open the glass to the deck. The plexi-dome capping the rotunda was tinted pinkish-yellow from the sun and it felt good to stand under its glow. I took a cleansing breath in through my nose, then held it for a long moment before slowly letting it out through my mouth. The dome seemed to breathe along with me, expanding and compressing like lungs as it regulated the oxygen of our living center. The deep vibration of the plexi was a perfect bass note to the piped-in tinkling of chimes. I took one more deep breath and set the basket down before pulling on my gloves. To protect against—what? And there my brain stalled as my healthy-mind kicked in, my years of training falling in step with my breath. Why worry about such things? Worry was a misuse of imagination, as a host once told me. It was best to forget why I should exercise caution when handling laundry, without ever forgetting that I should. We value mindfulness and positivity here at the center. Yes, laundry has to be done, but enjoy the moment. Live in the light, even in darkness. Find joy in your surroundings. Look out over the rotunda, but do not look down. Down is the past. Acknowledge other residents across the wide pit, standing on their decks, assessing the day, testing the air. Nod, smile. Take a breath. Give gratitude for the low volume of particulates in the air. Be thankful the power grid was working, without which we could not view our enlightened master in hologram form twice a day for meditation, but more important, power kept a floor of light suspended over the pit. If the grid went down the floor disappeared and the sight was horrific. There is no other word for it. If a blackout was expected to last more than a few hours, a giant canvas tarp has to be manually cranked over the dome to block out any natural light. Turning the rusty gears is not easy, but I crank with all the rest when need be. We put our own selves in darkness, but anything was better than seeing what was really there.

I remembered this guy, a real clown, someone new to the center, who, while we were turning the gears, told us that he thought the blackouts were done on purpose to keep us off balance. We had to kill him. But what was the point of remembering that? I brought my buzzing mind back with a few breaths, then tightened the gloves around my wrists. It was the perfect balance. I could attain equilibrium at will. My mind was my thoughts and my thoughts created who I was. As the master often told us, "You can decide what to think about. It's all up to you."

It wasn't until I reached for the basket that I noticed Doniker out on his deck, abutting my own. "Oh," I said. "Oh."

He sat so still on his meditation pillow he seemed to be part of the building. Stillness was good. Most predators cannot spot their prey unless it moves. They see not the thing itself, but the motion. I hoped I hadn't already disturbed him. His eyes were open as he stared out into the middle distance. He was centering well, but he did not look well. He had developed a bluish cast since I'd last seen him. When was that? When was the last time we could go outside? Again, I sensed my thoughts wandering and brought them back to my breath before I tripped myself up.

In. Hold. And release.

I only wished the weather could stay the way it was so Doniker could sit outside long enough to repair his damaged cells. But there was no point in wishing. It was going to be whatever it was going to be. Worry got you exactly nowhere. A trainer I once worked with taught me that worry was only a way to pretend you had control over what you don't. Amen to that.

I let Doniker be and went back to my laundry, bending with intention as I pawed through the basket. My head was lower than my heart, something we should strive for a few times a day, both physically and spiritually. "Lead with the heart, not with the brain," as the master always says. The plexi flexed and the chimes tinkled, but there was no human sound. All of us seemed as lost in our thoughts as Doniker. It was tempting to just hold my position but there was work to do. The laundry—my best calico tunic, my worst pants, my wool foot coverings, and the fine, impermeable film I wore against my skin—was tumbled together like a single wet creature. Taking care to keep my spine aligned, I stood up straight holding a damp foot covering. It was just like the ones on my feet, but clean, washed in the distilled rainwater collected from the dome and pumped right to the tub inside.

It was such an improvement from what it had been like before. What misery that had been, but I did not allow my thoughts to linger in that grim place. It could only drag me down. I glanced over at Doniker and took a deep, mindful breath. I clipped one foot covering on the rigging, then the other. The structural wires crisscrossed the domed rotunda from every one of the hundreds of cubes to another. A beautiful metaphor. "Think of your minds going out on silver cords," the master once said. "If you can separate your consciousness from your body, all you wonderful souls will be connected by energy."

And yet, here we were hanging laundry on those silver cords, because really, what else could we do?

A child warbled, the one who lived in the floor below. One of only two at the center. I got on my knees and squinted between the deck planks to see if the parents might let it out. It was so exciting to see a living, breathing young human instead of the jars some couples kept on their shelves. I wondered if it oughtn't to be in some other, special place, to be on the safe side. For the child's sake, and for ours. A child sighting could trigger all sorts of useless emotions in even the most resolute. It was hard not to think of the future when confronted with the young, making it difficult to tend to the balancing act of the mind. To be wholly in the present. There was nothing to be gained by looking back in nostalgia, and everything to be lost by looking forward with dread. As was stressed in our training, the mind can live in the past, it can project into the future, but it can only process the now. I was here now. I was fine now. I counted my breath to pull myself back to the moment.

In. Hold. Release. Again.

"Mariclaire?"

"Oh. Oh, Doniker."

He did not look my way. I crawled over to him. We were separated by a wall of wire mesh, and I leaned in close and spoke through it.

"Hi, Doniker. It's good to see you outside."

"Mariclaire," he whispered, his eyes still focused on a point in the middle of the rotunda, exactly where the master would appear later for centering down, helping us shut out our worldly cares for the night, complete with sedating incense and the hypnotic hum of chants and singing bowls. "Mariclaire," Doniker said again, and my mind snapped back to the present.

"What is it Doniker? I'm right here."

"Good-bye," he said, still not looking at me. "I'm dying."

That was a shock. I counted my heart beats for a full minute before speaking. "We're all dying," I said, forcing a chuckle. "Do you mean to say you're dying right now?"

He didn't answer, nor did he move his eyes or change his focus. He was already far along.

"Should I do something?" I asked, my voice betraying the knot of bile I felt rising in my throat. "Do you want me to help you?"

He did not respond. I looked around the rotunda, but all the people who had been outside just a moment before were gone. Could it be healthy nourishment time already? I hadn't heard the gates open. It didn't matter, there was no way I could leave now. This was my duty. I'd been called upon to spot Doniker, to make sure his transition went well. I began mumbling a mantra that a trainer had taught me long ago: *Panic may cause the situation to get worse. Panic may cause the situation to get worse. Panic may cause...* The proscribed steps came to me, and I lowered my voice. "Doniker, should you go get your Kit? It can help..."

He shook his head, no.

"You're not in pain?"

He shook no again, and I felt my breathing slow, returning to normal.

"Then you're probably not dying," I said. "Are you concentrating on your breath? That will get rid of any feelings of impending doom."

His head lowered in response and his gaze shifted down to the hologram floor of the rotunda. He seemed to be seeing right through it. Why would he do that to himself? He was too young. Mid-twenties, at that. He still had his hair. I didn't want to seem judgmental, but he had not rebounded from the loss of his wife the year before. He had not worked hard enough on processing his grief and moving on. I'd watched as he'd tenderly placed her body into the platform chute, the same foul place where our urine-soaked shavings and other messes were swept off each day. He cried openly when she disappeared through the hologram floor, and our eyes locked when we heard her land in the absorbent muck below. He had not really been himself ever since. He paced day and night. It did not speak well of his character or his training. It was a wonder he'd been allowed to stay.

"I'm hanging laundry," I said. "If you want me... If you want me to do anything, anything at all, I'm right here."

I stood up and clipped a piece of impermeable sheath to the rigging, then lifted my tunic from the damp pile, but the fabric began to separate from its own saturated weight. Using my most gentle touch, I tried to extricate it from the tangle of other wet things, but the more I pulled, the more it disintegrated in my hands. I had let it sit too long. The acidity of the water had already begun its work and there was no stopping it.

"Damn," I muttered.

"Don't," whispered Doniker, and he closed his eyes.

"Oh. Sorry. Sorry about that negativity. It was just... It was just that I really liked that tunic."

Doniker groaned and his chin fell to his chest.

"I know I shouldn't get so attached," I said. "I know that only leads to a world of hurt."

A shadow passed over the dome, a flying, living thing. And then it was gone. Before I knew it, tears burned on my cheeks. Breathe in. Exhale. Hold. Again. Count the breath. Count some more. If Doniker was determined to leave there was nothing to be done. There was no point in focusing on a problem when there was no solution. It was what it was.

"Doniker?" I said, but he did not respond. His color had gotten worse. He did, in fact, seem to be dying in the here and now, not in some abstract future. My pulse accelerated. I had never done this on my own before, assisting in a death-affirming action. It was harder than I could have imagined. I began to sway back and forth, then sideways, a self-comforting trick I'd learned along the way. Maybe I should go inside and get my own Kit, and find something in it to ease his transition. But by the time I ran in and got it, he could be gone, and I had an obligation to stay with him. That was the most important thing. To be with him now.

The wire fence between us could not be accessed, so I got back on my knees to be eye level with him and that's when I noticed some corroded mesh. With the clever use of a clothespin I was able to pry apart enough wire for a hole big enough for my arm. After weighing the consequences, and there were many, I removed my glove and squeezed my arm through the opening, pressing my torso hard against the wire, extending my arm until I could touch his shoulder.

"I'm here, Doniker," I said. "It's Mariclaire." My training kicked in and I began to breathe slowly and deeply from the abdomen, concentrating on a long out-breath and letting the in-breath take care of itself. It would all take care of itself. We stayed like that for a good while, his breaths coming weaker and further apart. I could hear gurgling in his chest. In time, the mediation bell sounded and gymnasts began swooping through the rigging, each on their own delicate trapeze, signaling everyone to come out of their cubes and onto their decks. Usually we meditated from behind our glass walls, but it was, as foretold, almost perfect weather. Funambulists skittered across the wires with their thuribles of smoke preparing the way for the master. A pinprick of white light began to pulsate under the dome and began to expand, brighter and bigger, filling the center of the rotunda, where the master slowly and completely materialized, a Tibetan singing bowl in his lap. He was rotating a leather mallet along the rim, producing the range of tones needed to restore our vibratory frequencies and bring us into harmony.

With a few breaths of absolute attention to the sounds, I attained the no-mind we all craved, and it was just at the moment I was about to drift off, Doniker's earthly weight began to tug at him. His realm was shifting. As we had been taught in the rare event we might want to release ourselves from our bodies, he had arranged himself to fall forward towards his open chute, head first. With a blinding flash, the hot white light was on us and the master was directing the center's attention to Doniker's journey. "We do not leave this world," he intoned ever so softly. "We only go back to it."

There was an expectant hush. As Doniker slid from my touch,

I grasped hold of his tunic, unwilling to let him go but he continued to fold away from me. The protective film on his shoulder fell, exposing his bare flesh, revealing a tattoo so small only I could see.

Resist.

Oh, Doniker. Poor boy. You spent all your energy with struggle, when, with a little more training, you could have learned to breathe through it. The tunic unraveled in my bare palm as he gently fell onto the chute, a transition of merciful seamlessness. He slid down its short distance, and then, abruptly, went into a stunning freefall, four limbs akimbo. The audience gasped as Doniker disappeared through the bright hologram floor and into the pit, and it was just at that moment our compassionate master clanged sharply on the singing bowl so we would not have to hear him land.

It Won't
Be Long Now

AT FIRST BELINDA fought against the strangling sheets, then heaved herself upright, alert to the point of fear. "What?" she asked, a variation on the question she usually asked to no avail: "Why?" There had been a prolonged wail, she was sure. Maybe. It was silent now. In the dark, the blinking red light on the monitor told her the unit was on, but not whether her daughter was breathing. She tried to slow her heartbeat to the machine's pulse, and hoped it had been just a fitful dream. Just. But she heard the pained cry again, seeming to come from all directions at once. She could not locate it even as she stumbled across the hall to Rowan's room. At the open door she held her breath and listened without turning on the light. She could hear blood pulse in her temples, but otherwise, nothing. No life-or-death fight for air going on here. Not this time.

She gathered herself together in the doorway, where for so many nights she'd slept on her feet like a horse. It had been a warm September and wet besides. The humid air that made the toilet paper damp and magazines curl, encouraged the spores that were her daughter's mortal foes. Single-celled creatures that didn't even know if they were animal or vegetable could take her down like gunshot. Belinda kept a trigger list on the refrigerator, but it might as well say "The World." Not only mold and mildew spores, but pollen from trees, grasses, and weeds, exercise, exposure to cold dry air or hot humid air, industrial emissions, vehicle exhaust, smog, and other air pollutants. *Strong emotions.* How could she protect her daughter from feelings? It would be easier to hold back the sea with a rope.

A dog bayed from across the mudflats, and Belinda snapped out of herself and crept to Rowan's side. Her breathing was raspy but steady, and Belinda's shoulders eased. Her own breathing was still labored, but that was because of all the lard she carried around her "mid-section" as her doctor called it, like she was a cut of beef. She hated the needy part of herself that made her reach for food when her own strong emotions had her by the throat. The night-light shone on Rowan, lighting up one side of her buttery, plump face. Ten years old and already "obese" as they said in school. Now there was a word gone awry in the system. It used to be reserved for problem fatties, now it was attached to kids like Rowan who were merely on the pudgy side. Some of that—maybe a lot of that—was because Belinda was afraid exercise would trigger an asthma attack so she kept her out of sports. No lean athletic body for Rowan. Not like her dad, the robust one. Yet he was the one who didn't make it. Jim was a fisherman in a fished-out sea. His captain had been forced to go farther and farther out to catch anything at all, in all weather. On a day the birds were blown inside out like umbrellas, Jim got snagged by a line and swept off the deck. The crew tried, but Jim never came up once. Not once. After a few unfathomable words from the Coast Guard, her future dissolved like salt in water. She buried an empty coffin and called him dead.

Belinda did not want to wake Rowan, but she could not resist a single touch. She let her palm drop on her child's chest, just to feel it rise. Rowan's shoulder was moist beneath her Little Mermaid nightgown, and while Belinda pondered what that might mean, the Banshee wail rose up again and she pulled her hand away as if she'd been stung by a jellyfish. But the unearthly sound hadn't come from her daughter, or even from inside the house. It—a deer? coyote?— was in the backyard. The noise was so alien it could even be a bear. They hadn't been seen in coastal Massachusetts in a hundred years, but then again, neither had coyotes, and yet they'd recently returned as suburban pests. Nothing seemed impossible anymore when it came to nature. But whatever "it" was, it was in trouble. The barks and gasps were like the worst of Rowan's attacks, the ones that sent them to the ER for a few hours on the nebulizer.

Rowan rolled over with a grunt, but did not wake up. Belinda tip-toed out of the room and back to her own. She looked at the clock. Four a.m. The hour of the wolf, as Jim used to say, the time he got up nearly every day of his life. She pulled a sweatshirt over her head and stood at the window, staring out into the gray world of the salt marsh where no artificial light reflected off the water. The moon was long gone. The plaintive moans continued so there was no use trying to get back to sleep. She held the nylon curtain like a security blanket against her face and waited for the sun to catch up with her. The outbursts continued, less frequently but more disturbing, like something out of a horror movie. "What *are* you?" she asked. A young animal calling for its mother? An old one pushing hard against the inevitable?

In time, the first yellow glow of the sun began to organize the yard into light and dark. She watched featureless birds shake themselves awake in the branches and fly off. The house cast a long shadow. By the fence, the sunlight fell on the broken swing set with its cracked slide and Rowan's turtle-shaped sandbox, things she'd long outgrown but they had not known how to get rid of. The same with the lobster boat up on a wooden cradle. It was shrouded in a tarp streaked with gull shit, and the keel was hairy with dried green slime. A boat out of water was a sorry thing. Belinda kept putting it on Craigslist, hoping for a nibble, but it was too far gone. Jim had bought it cheap to fix up and start lobstering, since apparently there were still bugs for the catching. Mostly though, he wanted to stay closer to shore for Rowan's sake. So much for that.

She realized that the sound had become silent, and the silence was nothing short of ominous. The sun rose higher, making the house shadow shorter, letting her see farther down where the yard began to morph into tidal marsh. She squinted her eyes. "What the…?" A black lumpen form. A giant trash bag? It was too far up on the lawn to have come floating in at high tide. Maybe someone got rid of a dog, or even a litter of puppies, tossed like garbage in her yard. It made her sick to her stomach. She was glad it was Saturday so she could take care of it one way or another before Rowan woke up. She didn't want her to know the worst about the world.

She pulled her shell pants on over her pajama bottoms and slipped on Jim's old rubber boots. They were too big, but they worked, and she could not afford to replace anything that still worked. Her job at the diner paid for shit. The little bit of insurance money had run out, and she was wearing out her welcome at the Fisherman's Widows & Orphans Fund. She closed the back door quietly behind her and picked her way down the slope towards the marsh. There had been a mean downpour a few days before. The lawn still squished with the weight of her step. The air had that murky morning stink, and the shadows were so dense she was surprised she could even walk through them.

She stopped at the woodpile to grab a stick of kindling, just in case. There was plenty of it. Their poorly insulated house had been mostly heated by wood, with just a few electric baseboard heaters that she could not afford to turn on. But Rowan's doctor said no more wood stove. "How can she be allergic to wood smoke?" she'd asked him. "Didn't humans evolve with it? Didn't fire jump-start civilization?" He'd shrugged. "Maybe we're devolving," he'd said, with a chuckle. This was the same doctor who told her to get air-conditioning to keep Rowan from coughing up garden slugs, but he did not tell her how to pay for it.

Holding onto her stick, she approached the bag with caution. In the half-hearted light, she saw the bag move. She stopped about twenty feet away. She hadn't thought about how she could safely open the bag. She patted her pants. No phone. That was dumb. As she was wondering if she should just go back and call the police, the pointy end of the bag lifted up and stared at her with mournful eyes.

"A seal? Are you a harbor seal?" She looked around as if the answer were to be found in the reeds. It was far from home, sep-arated from the sea by miles of marsh. She turned back to this baby-faced animal, still not quite believing it. "What are you doing here?" The seal lowered its head, but kept its eyes on her as she inched closer. His dove-gray body was mostly neck and chest, and his head was like a peeled egg with whiskers. As she got closer still, she caught the scent of deep ocean on him, the way Jim used to smell at the end of a long trip.

She stood still, not knowing quite what to do, and as the sun rose, she saw that the seal had deep cuts all over its body and his stomach was raw. "Poor thing," she said. He must have been pulling his blubber on land for some distance. If he was not exactly dying, he was as near to it as to make no matter. She took a step towards it, still clutching her stick, and it lunged towards her with a snap of its yellow teeth.

She jumped back. "Okay! I get it." Because of Rowan, she'd been so used to seeing seals as cute plush toys or cartoon figures, she'd forgotten what they were really like. At the town dock, they lounged on their backs eating live lobsters they'd stolen from traps, holding the struggling crustaceans between two flippers like ice cream cones, crunching through the shells with a bite that could tear off your face.

A man from the Aquarium, with rimless glasses and a dense beard, looked down towards the estuary. The sky was an even dead white, and the air was warm. It was autumn only by the falling leaves of the swamp maples. "He hauled himself all the way up here?"

Belinda shrugged. "He started making a fuss sometime after I went to bed. I thought it was a human crying or something."

"They can be like that." A woman from the rescue team put down her satchel. "When explorers first landed on Cape Cod, the sailors thought the seals were mermaids, calling to them."

"Want to hear a mermaid joke?" asked Rowan, shyly.

Belinda wished Rowan had stayed up at the house. The yard

was lousy with wet leaves, and she could smell the spores bloom-ing at their feet. The "Aspergillus monster" she and Rowan called the fungus. Besides which, this whole thing might end poorly. But how could she keep her from seeing the seal? Rowan loved animals, yet they could not have a dog, and a cat was out of the question. And here, an animal appears right in her yard. A sick animal, but a real one.

"Shoot." The woman studied the seal with a squint, walking around its six-foot tapered body. She was almost as tall as the seal was long, but thin as an eel. She wore jeans and a t-shirt and was so tan she had sunburnt eyelids. Belinda was glad she'd made the effort to change out of her dumpy sweats and put on a nice shirt and jeans, even though they were so tight she could barely breathe and the phone in her pocket dug into her hips. She even put on her good sneakers, knowing they'd get soaked in the grass. For some reason, she had wanted to make a good impression on these people. Same as Rowan, apparently.

"Okay," said Rowan, squeezing her hands together. "A man and a cat are on a desert island. They see a mermaid on a rock. The man imagines the mermaid as having a pair of legs, and the cat imagines her as all fish." The tanned woman laughed, causing Rowan to squeal with delight. Belinda worried laughing would lead to coughing.

"That's a good one," said the bearded man. "We only see what we need, don't we?"

A man in a hoodie and flip-flops was crouched down near the seal. "Maybe we should just put him out of his misery," he said. "He's in a pretty bad way." Belinda made a face at him and shook her head.

"Misery?" said Rowan, softly.

"Why is it here?" asked Belinda, to switch the subject.

"Look." The woman pointed to its tail. "Fishing filament wrapped around his hindflippers and tail."

"You know what the monkey said when it backed his tail into the lawn mower?" asked Rowan. Everyone stared at her. "It won't be long now."

"That's not funny," said Belinda. The two men made polite ha-ha mutterings and went about their business, but the woman looked concerned, obviously wondering what child would joke in response to a distressed animal. Rowan had developed a sick sense of humor since Jim died. Her counselor at school told Belinda it was her way of distancing herself from pain.

"The seal couldn't use his flippers to swim," the woman explained, as if Rowan's problem was that she hadn't understood the situation. "Looks like he got pretty battered when the tide pulled him in through the marsh channels. It's a wonder he didn't drown."

"He can't drown," said Rowan. "He lives in the water."

"He's a mammal, like us," said the bearded man. "He can hold his breath longer, but he still has to come up for air. If he can't swim, he sinks."

"Probably why he was trying to escape above the tide line," said flip-flop boy. "He's a fighter, I have to give him that."

"Well, let's give him a chance then," said the bearded man, dialing a number on his phone. The tips of his fingers were flat, like a frog's. "I'm going to try to snag a boat and move him that way. He'll be less stressed. Besides, we'll never get the rescue unit out of this muck if we bring it down here."

"Then someone would have to rescue the rescue unit, right?" said the tan woman, making Rowan giggle. "Let's get this line off him first. Jason, go get the halter."

"Will he get better?" asked Rowan.

"We'll see what we can do for him at the Aquarium," said the woman. "He might just need a few stitches and some rest."

Belinda didn't believe a word of it. None of them looked as if they really expected it to live. The seal was watching them, and Belinda thought there was a wordless intelligence behind those big eyes that knew it too.

The bearded man put his phone away. "The harbor master will meet us at the dock. He's got a sweet little inflatable with a lift for us, but he said we might have to wait a bit for the tide to turn to enter the marsh."

Jason came back with a canvas halter, letting it slip over the seal, tightening the straps to keep it still. It did not lunge at them the way it had gone at Belinda, and she was a little put out by that. The

woman slipped on rubber gloves that went up to her elbows, protective goggles, and a surgical mask. The kind Rowan had to wear
on high pollen days.

"What are you afraid of catching?" Belinda asked, alarmed about
a possible new danger for Rowan.

The woman took a pair of curved scissors out of her satchel.
"It's not for me. It's to protect the seal from any germs *I* might have.
He's got a lot of open sores." She began to snip away the tangle of
line. "What a mess. I think there's a hook embedded too." The seal
twitched, and Jason was having some trouble controlling him.

"This is all we've done for days," said the bearded man, grabbing one of the straps to help Jason. Belinda pulled Rowan back.
"A storm out to sea worked up these lines that just float around
catching sea mammals like our buddy here. Mostly we've just been
counting the dead."

As the Aquarium people worked, Belinda was touched that
they would go to all this trouble to try to save him. She ought to try
as hard to save herself. She looked around at the broken toys and
unused boat, the vinyl clapboards peeling off the back of the house.
Belinda became painfully aware of how shabby her life must look to
them. Since Jim died over a year ago, she had not kept up with the
repairs of the house. She had not taken care of so many things, and
now it was all falling down around her. Maybe these people were
thinking they would have to rescue her as well as the seal.

Rowan coughed and then tried to stifle the next. She took her inhaler out of her pocket and took a hit, then another.

"Come on, you," Belinda said to Rowan. "Grandma's going to be here soon to pick you up."

Her parents both smoked, so Rowan could never go to their house, but they went on road trips sometimes. Today there were going to the mall to buy some school things, and knew not to smoke in the car with Rowan. They learned that lesson the hard way. Belinda was going to go along, but now she thought she'd stay and make sure things went smoothly with the seal. Maybe she could be of some help.

"Just stay away from the seal while we're gone," said flip-flop boy. "He wants to rest, and a human presence could send him over the edge."

"Don't worry," said Belinda, once again feeling a little put out. It was her seal after all. It was her yard. "Rowan's off for the day with her grandma and I've got work to do around the house."

"What?" asked Rowan. "What work? I thought you were coming with us."

"Off we go!" said Belinda, patting her daughter on the bum to get her moving. They hiked back up the slope to the house, neither of them breathing pretty.

In the end, Belinda couldn't help herself. After Rowan and her parents drove off, having explained to her mom, yet again, how to use the emergency call feature on Rowan's phone, she sat at the kitchen table with a coffee mug and looked out the window. The tide was slack and the seal was quiet. Maybe he was feeling better now that the line had been cut away from his tail. Or maybe he'd just given up.

"You must be hungry," she said out loud. She heaved herself out of the chair and made two tuna sandwiches, one for her, and one for him, stacking them on a paper plate. She found Rowan's unbreakable cereal bowl and covered the sandwiches with it, then grabbed a plastic water bottle out of the refrigerator and tucked it under her arm. "Okay, then," she said, and carried the picnic down to her salty visitor.

She was still wearing her sneakers, so she slipped a bit on the wet lawn going down to the marsh. The seal seemed to study her progress, wondering how a land animal could be so clumsy on land. She squatted close to him, but not too close. She remembered his pointy teeth. As she bent, she felt the waistband of her jeans slice into her flesh, so she unsnapped her top button and released her breath. "That's better," she said. She threw one of the tuna sandwiches to the seal, half expecting it to catch it mid-air like at Sea World, but it landed in pieces by his clawed flippers. She poured some water into the bowl and pushed it towards him with the piece of kindling, getting it as close as she dared. The seal gave her a look of warning and she backed off, settling herself on the ground well out of reach. She wished she'd brought a folding chair with her. The ground was damp and she was not sure she could stand back up without help. She had to take her phone out of her pocket and put it next to her in order to get comfortable at all.

She dug into her sandwich but the seal did not even look at his. "I know," she said, chewing. "I wish I had chips too. Maybe a pickle." But it wasn't funny. He seemed worse off than before, even without the fishing line. He wasn't moving and didn't blink. Maybe flip-flop boy was right, and he was too far gone after all.

Belinda finished her lunch in a few bites and sighed. It was sad about the seal, but it was nice to be outside doing nothing. She rarely got to just sit. The warmth of the day made her sleepy. Even the wind was drowsy. Nearby was a circle of smooth beach stones with a charred center, all that was left of a few fine summer evenings, where, if Rowan stayed upwind of the smoke, they would sit outside and consider the stars. But the last time they'd had a campfire, Rowan had woken up in the middle of the night in trouble, so they hadn't done it since. It was getting so Rowan could no longer take part in the natural world. Maybe they should do what the doctor suggested and move to Arizona, where the desert air was too dry for spores, and the schools were air-conditioned. But Belinda couldn't imagine leaving this place. It was all she knew.

She looked at the seal. The tuna sandwich sat untouched,

attracting flies, some of which began to settle on his wounds. She slowly stretched towards him to wave them away with her paper plate and he bared his teeth at her. His breath smelled like a ship's hold and she stopped. She wanted to say she was sorry—about the fishing line, about the flies, about everything—but he did not want her sympathy.

"Suit yourself," she said. It's what she got for trying to help. She should just leave him alone and go back to the house, but some instinct would not let her leave his side. He was stranded, just like her. She was a bit seal-shaped herself, with almost the same number of chins. They were both full-blooded mammals, distant cousins, for better or worse. Here was a species who used to live on land but had decided against it. For some reason, the seals had chosen to go back to the sea. She wondered if they regretted that decision, now that the water was getting as dangerous for the seal as the land was for Rowan. In the meantime, the die was cast for them all. If he survived, he would return to his element. She imagined him healed and healthy, striking out for the sea, pushing himself along the sand with his muscular flippers, then merging with the water as if he and it were one.

Belinda wondered if going back would ever be an option for humans. It had not been an option for Jim. She flashed on his death, as she so often did, his leg caught in the tangle of lines, the frightening change from air to water, him twirling in the green gloom, the panic as he tried to reach for the knife in his belt, then the horrific awareness that it was too late. The vastness of the ocean was nothing compared to the finality of death. She hoped he experienced a moment of beauty before it all went dark, that he felt embraced by the water, swimming in love, as if he were coming home at last.

"Life is a struggle against death, my friend," she said to the seal. The light was dimming. The rescue team had better hurry, what with the days getting shorter. She looked at the marsh, and the water seemed high enough for the boat to enter the channel. "Soon," she said to the seal. "Very soon." Her mind became silent as she stared at him, admiring the perfect arched line of his body, the puppy-dog eyes. He was truly a beautiful being of the sea. When he turned his head away from her, she did what they told her not to do. She shuffled closer to him on her butt, then reached over and touched him.

Who knew such a large animal could move so fast? She felt the bite in slow-motion, the slice through her muscles, teeth against bone, veins and arteries opening wide to the world, coloring it red. The pain was so vivid it did not even register. When she got free, she hugged her arm to her body and would not look at it. The seal was more alert than he'd been all day, arching back like a snake. She felt warmth soak through her shirt and spread across her stomach, and she lay down on her side.

Fear deadened her voice. She could not cry out for help, but she could hear everything with a clarity she hadn't even know existed.

Off in the distant harbor, the sound of the sea was a breathing thing. She heard the peals of church bells in town, the brass sound reverberating softer and softer until it was just a whisper. Then she realized that it was not a church bell, but her phone, lying in the weedy grass, vibrating and flashing red. She envisioned her mother in the ER with Rowan, but could not pick it up. She would meet them soon enough. She heard the mechanical hum of the boat as it hydroplaned over the marsh, and the great marsh birds flapping away at its coming. She could almost smell its exhaust. She imagined the blades of the boat's propeller cutting through the water towards her, and the spray rising up to the sky in front of the prow, the vessel leaving a splendid hollow in its wake. "We're saved," she whispered to the seal, even though she didn't believe a word of it. "Saved."

She closed her eyes, and in the darkness the animal heaved itself just that much closer and made a noise that pierced her soul. Her dry mouth formed the question "Why?" as if she did not already know.

Infant

Kettery

THE THIRST. THE trembling, heaving thirst. Struggling neurons firing out of control, toxic puddles running down the raw membranes of his throat. The shakes a hot electric current pulsing through his body. The iron taste of blood on his parched lips, wet ashes between the teeth. Roiling dreams of monstrous flare-ups, him, him, the unlucky endling, trying to squelch the ravenous dragon with the only weapon on hand, the treasured sips of vodka, which only fed the flames. Pure energy, the vodka. The dragon morphing into a single organism oozing over the planet devouring it, licking it clean with hot scarlet tongues flickering endlessly from its mouth. Slobbering with fire. Les left his burning body for the skies, creating distance, soaring outside the Virgo Supercluster of galaxies before looking back at Earth, seeing the monster whole for what it was. Us. The dragon was us. He knew what had to be done. A sacrifice was called for and his eyes flashed open in horror. He was the one. It was coming for him.

Weeds and parched flowers came into focus. Near his face a brown spider spun a web suspended between two thistle stems, working its spinnerets, letting out the lovely silk from its ass. The gossamer web was as intricate and perfect as what? His mind? As his mind used to be? Or will be? The beautiful web with a deathly purpose. What was to be trusted? A spider had to eat, like Les had to drink. The spider was born already knowing its job, its short life driven by purpose, but Les had a hard time waking up no matter where he put his head, even in this place of all silence, the cemetery. His first awakening in the arroyo that morning was very bad, very bad, all wild noise and panic. A skin-tight cow had stumbled into the arroyo, her thirst driving her into the trap. No water. None in any months, but in her bowed head a rushing creek of sweet memory. The withered beast didn't have the strength to climb back out, and after a number of scrambles and dusty falls simply lay down in the sun and offered herself up to the deer flies. Les tried to help. They all tried. But no coaxing, no pulling or pushing by the small group could get her back on all fours again. Three different people went to town looking for help and never came back. One older woman, two tea-colored children clinging to her legs, collected small donations of water in a bowl and offered it to her but no go. Too late. Much too late. Could not even lift her head. Her eyes gaped up at the sky, searching for her heavenly herd in the clouds, dreaming of the golden calves before her.

"You can only help those who want help," said the woman with the water. She carried the bowl away, her children dotted with splash. One by one, the others gave up hope and left. Les stayed. Death was inevitable. Dying alone was not.

"We are in this together, my sweet bovine." He stroked the fur on her head, and brushed the flies away from her open mouth. "The truth is, Bessie, we're all just a few steps behind you."

Les sat crouched on his heels by the cow's head for an hour or more, a human presence, the very smell of which kept the coyotes at bay so they would not eat the old girl alive. Not that it looked like she'd notice. She was so far gone the film on her dark brown eyeballs had dried. And yet the ribs continued to rise. How had she gotten separated from her herd? From the looks, she'd been untended for a while, her milk bags long gone dry, her societal structure torn away. Why hadn't the farmer gone looking for her? Even old sick cows were worth money to pet food companies. An escapee from a meat processing plant? He knew the feeling. She wanted to die under the open sky, not the abattoir. He opened his arms to the world, such as it was in the trash-strewn arroyo.

"Here it is, old girl. Have at it."

And soon the heaving breath moved from the ribs to the throat, first struggling, then hoarse, then imperceptible, then gone. The big circle turns. He could not explain his tears, but someone had to pony up for this magnificent creature, gone from the earth, a feast for scavengers. The coyotes paced in the shadows of the dry brush, waiting for him to leave. Farther down the arroyo he saw others waiting, men wondering whether they should beat the coyotes to the corpse, women wondering how the cow could be transformed into food.

Waking up sucked big time. Yet because of sip naps he had cause to wake several times a day. This time in the cemetery. Les rolled his body over to his heart side, then hauled himself to a sitting position with pained effort, coordinating elbows and knees, finding leverage, gaining altitude, until he felt his upper body press firmly against a gravestone then let his head fall back to open the airways. Look. The sky. Still there. A cloud is only water, but arranged like none other, the molecules refracting light in heavenly shapes. The sun declined behind the Rockies, the continent's primordial spine, and infused the cemetery with a reddish western light, a jagged shadow edging closer to where he sat, the quilted cirrocumulus stretching low and thin above him, vibrating with mango light. It was a glorious thing to witness. Like the death of the cow, it was a fleeting wonder. It would not be long before climate change annihilated all the cows on the land and the clouds in the sky, burning them off in a warmer atmosphere. No more shafts of divine light falling through the billowing cumulous, a sad end to the biblical concept of God in the heavens. We are the destroyer of gods. Zeus was right, humans could not be trusted with fire. Prometheus should not have given it to us, a species destined to abuse its power. He deserved to have his liver devoured, over and over.

Speaking of liver. He patted his garments for the familiar pint, took a sip and sent warm blood through his dry veins. He got out of the science biz just in time. Knowledge can not help us for what we are about to experience. A no-narrative future with no precedence. He stared at the trembling hand that held the bottle. In his dream he'd seen his hands, torn and swollen, the skin falling off in sheets. It was supposed to be good luck to see one's own hands in a dream, but how is that luck? Maybe that he still had the eyes to see them.

He put the bottle in his jacket pocket then ran his hands through his matted hair, his braid coming loose in his fingers. He pulled up a pants leg to examine his latest sores and scabs. He bruised as easily as an old peach these days. He couldn't be trusted on pavement, but he had to work on Pearl if he wanted his sips. It had been a good day on the pedestrian mall. An excellent day. He'd painted a new sign, "The universe provides. Be the universe." Soon he had enough for more than a few sips, he earned a whole pint, sending him off to where he sat now, Boulder's Columbia cemetery, to rest the ceaseless storm of neural firings in his head.

The world gets mad at the drunk for not being able to change the behavior that might kill him, yet the world is unable to change the behavior that is killing itself. He took a long swig and swished it around in mouth before swallowing. He tucked the bottle away in the dark folds of his clothes and felt a small lump. Tumor? No, a totem. A stone in the bottom of a pocket. It came back to him now. While he sat with the cow, he found a fossil in the dust near her head. The faint impressions of a shell, from when the Rocky Mountains were at the bottom of the sea, before two ancient tectonic plates collided and became one, under God, indivisible. What forms had that calcium taken over the course of its geological history? It might have travelled through the bones of dinosaurs and now here it is, in his own very hand.

He placed it tenderly on top of the gravestone next to him, which was so sunk into the ground it was about level with the earth. He looked at the faded lettering. Infant Kettery, Aged One Day, August 1870. No name. No gender. He turned to read the stone he leaned upon. Not a Kettery. No other Kettery around. The baby alone. A transient. Well, babycakes, aren't we all? Infant Kettery was probably conceived in the east only to be born here on the westward expansion. Maybe too soon. An unsustainable burden. Weak. Needy. The mother forced to make a harsh assessment of time and resources needed to cross the Divide before winter, and decided, no. No. The survival of the family unit had to be considered. The other families were giving each other the eye. Her husband turned his back and looked up at the stars. All their energy had to be directed to the difficult crossing, where, on the other side, land awaited. They were all eager to start claiming property, confronting any indigenous nations in their path. A new beginning with no room at the inn for tenderness. The milk never flowed. No other lactating mother stepped forward. The infant cried, whimpered, then went silent. After a short delay, the family must have continued their migration, moving up and on, away from their grief, climbing the Divide, leaving a small, still bundle in the ground behind them. There was no looking back. There was no looking inwards. There was only looking ahead. This was America after all. The future beckoned.

He pulled his bottle out of his pocket, emptied it and closed his eyes. Wet with tears.

This grieving, this constant grieving. How will it end?

Flying Home

SHELLEY WOKE TO a high-pitched sound and braced herself for a nurse to come swooping in to see if she was dead. She wondered if that's how she was going to know it was over, with one long shrill beep. But the door did not open in a flurry of protective polyester, and at any rate, the sound had stopped. The machines that monitored her bodily functions seemed to be blinking and blurting with no special urgency. With great effort, and not a little pain, she turned her head to the window, smushing her oxygen mask against her temple. "Oh! Hello."

A red-tailed hawk was sitting on an iron rod that extended out from Boulder Community Hospital, right outside Shelley's room on the fourth floor. She'd noticed the rod before, when she first arrived another lifetime ago and had enough breath to stand up to look out the window and get her bearings in the world. A narrow side window was cracked open and it had felt good to feel honest-to-god Colorado air on her skin. But those few steps nearly did her in and the day nurse, Jeanette, looking like an astronaut in her baby-blue gear, had to help her back to bed. "Nice try, Shelley," she'd said. "But next time, you ring for me."

"I thought you'd say no," said Shelley.

"I will say no. That's why I say, ring for me. The last thing we need right now is a fall."

It was a moot point. After that, she never had the strength again. It took everything she had to breathe, but she was glad she got that one peek. If she hadn't, she might not know about the rod and then have to wonder what the hawk was sitting on, and it hurt her head to think. The rod was probably a leftover from some sloppy repair, but this big raptor seemed to think it was custom built for his own private perch. It was a good-looking bird with dark brown plumage and eponymous red tail, without which she'd be hard-pressed to say what kind of hawk it was. As it was, she didn't know her male from her female. The bird's intense, furrowed stare was aimed not at her—really, who would want to look at her now?—but at the utility courtyard below where there was a dumpster, and a dumpster meant rats. Probably plenty of them. Pickings were slim at restaurant dumpsters in town what with the lockdown, so rats across the city were starving, ravaging homes in search of food. Before she got sick she'd seen them out on the streets in broad daylight, taking risks, exposing themselves to danger in hopes of finding food. The hospital dumpster was a good bet for untouched meals. The medical staff didn't seem to have time to eat, and most Covid patients couldn't ingest anything other than fluids by way of an IV. She first suspected she had the virus was when she was making coffee and couldn't smell it. By the end of that day her temperature was over a hundred, and that night she was on her hands and knees trying to find a position where she could breathe. Eventually she crawled to her phone and called her son, who called 911.

Rats weren't the only ones interested in the dumpster. Crows, those vacuum cleaners with wings, were ripping their way beak and claw through plastic bags of cafeteria garbage, chattering away like shoppers. "Did you see this? Is there any more of that?" They soared across her view with the foul scrapings of hospital trays trailing from their beaks. It was a wonder they could get airborne they were so loaded. A baked potato shell, some strands of fettuccini, a gray strip of chicken skin. They certainly didn't want the red-tail staring down at them while they scavenged. It might get tired of waiting for a rat to dart out from the dumpster and choose one of them for lunch instead. It was a bird-eat-bird world. As she gazed at the hawk, a crow suddenly photo-bombed her view, trolling its nemesis with a swoop. But the hawk was unperturbed, and gave the crow a look that could have plucked him bald. "Stay strong, hawk," she muttered from under her mask. Just as her eyes began to flutter closed, the hawk pushed itself off the rod and shot down into the courtyard. She stretched her neck but she couldn't see if it scored a rat, and she never saw it rise.

Over the next few days the red-tail and the crows became her entertainment as she struggled to breathe, giving her something to think about other than cement lungs. The hawk showed up on the rod at least once a day, but she never knew when to expect it. The crows were a constant, noisy presence but were rarely in flight where she could see them. Sparrows, who were thugs in their own right, often flew by in intimidating masses. Sometimes she felt the place was a little over-birded, but they were visitors after all, something not allowed otherwise. Her son and his family came once, at a prearranged time, and the nursing staff helped her to a wheelchair so she could wave at them from the window. It was exhausting for everyone. Dave held little Bennie in his arms and pointed at her window, which was certainly too far up for them to see anything other than a shadow. His wife Betsy was with them, which was alarming. She must really be sick if her daughter-in-law felt she should come along. They stood between the dumpster and a white refrigerated trailer and waved while the crows looked down on them from the budding cottonwood trees, impatient to return. The birds bobbed their heads and flew from limb to limb, making the branches bounce as if the weight of elephants had been lifted. She looked over the crows and beyond the hospital wing to the foothills and the snow-capped Rockies in the distance. When was the last time she even noticed the mountains?

When she looked back down at her family, they seemed so small. Her only child, her only grandchild. Small, vulnerable mammals. Sometimes she wondered if humans had any purpose at all. Keith, her ex-husband, had said we were here to protect the earth but that made no sense. From what she could tell, the earth needed to be protected from us. In fact, she didn't see where humans fit anywhere in what he called the great web of life. We devoured everything but seemed to be no one's primary food source anymore, unless you counted the virus. In which case, we were toast.

Jeanette came up behind her. "Shelley, we've got to get you back in bed. Wave good-bye." Shelley raised an arm tethered by a blood pressure cuff, and she saw her son mouth something. She leaned to put her ear to the open sliver of window, but Jeanette pulled her back before she lost her balance. She should have charged her phone so they could talk, but, in truth, she didn't really have the breath, and her voice from under the mask would frighten Bennie. It certainly frightened her, but she was grateful it was just a mask and not a tube down her throat. That's what happened when they moved you from a regular Covid room, like hers, to the dreaded ICU. Endgame.

As Jeanette rolled her back to bed, she knew the moment her son and his family walked away because she heard the crows descend on the dumpster again in noisy celebration. She wished the window could open all the way so she could hear them better. The hospital walls were thick and her breathing filled her ears, not to mention electronic squawks and the noisy hallway. But no matter how loud it got inside, she could always tell when a custodian went outside with garbage because the crows made such a ruckus. A food delivery! And if she was at all awake she knew when the hawk was on his way because a military detail of crows often mobbed him, trying to keep him away from his perch. Once, she saw them escort the hawk off the hospital property. Crows were persistent little buggers. Another time, she woke just as the hawk rose up from the courtyard with a mighty flapping of wings, a limp rat dangling from its claws. As much as she'd been rooting for the hawk against the crows, she felt for the rat. She hoped the end was quick. Suffering was a terrible thing.

She remembered once, when she was down with the flu, Keith trying to get her to sit outside in bone-chilling February weather to boost her immune system, insisting that natural settings were healing and would create a path to her soul if only she were open to the experience. It was such a Boulder thing to say. He was as annoying as a crow sometimes, constantly soul-questing, always trying to improve himself, forcing her to come along. After they got divorced she never hiked again. What a brat she was. What she wouldn't do to be able to hike right now, to have that sort of breath. Funny she should think of him now. Those years began spooling out in front of her like colorful ribbons, the scenes vivid and magical like a movie, and she tried to grasp her younger, hopeful self to keep her from disappearing again. Somehow in the process, she pulled a tube from her arm, and Jeanette came in and loosely tied her hands to the bed with soft bandages, and that was surely for the best.

Later, she opened her eyes and there was a crow on the rod, looking in at her, first with one eye, then turning its beak to look at her with the other. Or was it a gargoyle? The creature was all beak and wing, hunched over and ugly, spouting words instead of rainwater. "Life is a near-death experience," it cackled before flying away.

Oh no. She was hallucinating now. That couldn't be good. What was that nursery rhyme about counting crows? One is for sorrow? There was some sort of commotion going on in the hallway. She side-eyed the hall window and there were gurneys everywhere, a traffic jam of the sick and dying. She was grateful to have a bed. She heard a man call out that he was a lawyer. "This situation is actionable," he croaked. "When this is over, there'll be hell to pay."

If only she had the oxygen to laugh.

When there were no birds to focus on, she stared off at the familiar peaks and sloughs of the mountains. Spring was coming. The snow was melting, exposing the scarred landscape along the slopes, still black with soot from the wildfires that fall. That had been a scary time. You couldn't breathe from the smoke and ash. There were other scary times. She remembered going up a trail together as a family and coming across a fresh kill. The bloody contents of a deer had been hollowed out and devoured, the insides ribbed like the roof of a cathedral. Eviscerated was the word. She was uneasy knowing there was some animal, drooling red, waiting for them to leave so it could finish the job. Keith hardly gave the deer a glance, except to remark on the different types of flies on the carcass, and kept on his steady pace to the top of the ridge, but she and Dave stopped to gape. He was only five. "What happened?" he asked.

"Life happened," she said. "It's sad, but the bear or mountain lion who killed the deer needed to live too."

Dave's eyes grew large. "Is it dead?"

It took a moment for Shelley to respond. What constituted dead if not this? And yet. The blood was wet and the flies pulsed with vitality, making it seem as if life was just moving from one form to another. "The deer is definitely dead," she'd said at last. "Look at it. It's all eaten away." He squatted to peer into the carcass, and a cloud of flies rose up. "Let's go," she said and grabbed his hand. They continued up the mountain, meeting up with Keith and then, after she begged, they took a different path back down. She told Keith it was for Dave's sake, but she knew it was for her own.

She'd do anything to hit that trail again, to be in the mountains where life could be reconsidered. To review all the options again. She'd felt like she'd been circling the drain for days, but at least someone had removed the bandages. Maybe the worst was over. Or maybe they had to untie her to flip her over onto her stomach to take the pressure off her lungs. That had seemed to help, but there was no more looking out the window, and the mask dug into her cheeks. A physical therapist came in to help her, as he called it, "visualize her breathing."

"Think of your shoulder blades as your wings," he'd said, putting his gloved hand on her bare back. "Now, pull your breath into your wings and feel them open. Expand your wings, Shelley. Good. Now let the breath go. Fold your wings and relax. Expand, and fold. Again. Good. Open your wings wide, Shelley. Excellent. You'll be flying in no time."

It was so Boulder. But it helped.

In between people coming and going to mess with her, she tried to sleep but the noise seemed to ramp up every time she closed her eyes. The beeps, the alarms, the announcements. Code this, code that. The crying out. The oxygen machine was so loud. Both she and the machine were working hard. She wished they'd turn it up. She heard people out in the hall say Covid this, Covid that. Wait. Or were they saying corvid? Corvid? She pressed her mind into action until it came up with the answer. A crow was a corvid! Counting corvids. Counting crows. Counting Covids. If a group of crows was called a murder, what was a group of Covids called? A slaughter. She laughed, but it used too much precious oxygen and she started gagging and Jeanette ran in with a syringe.

One is for sorrow,

Two is for mirth,

Three for a wedding,

And four for a death.

Later, after a team came to flip her right side up again, a nurse's aide brought her an iPad. "Someone wants to say hello." It was Dave and Bennie, and she sensed they weren't calling to say hello. Dave said he loved her too many times. They were falsely cheerful so she was falsely fine, then drifted off to sleep in the middle of a sentence. Wild visions, the sound of crows infiltrating everything. Humans in her dreams began to speak in caws and clacks. Telling corvid jokes. A corvid and a rabbi walk into a bar. Then Covid followed and they never walked out. No one laughed. This place has no fucking sense of humor.

At sunset, the crows were going wild and she opened her eyes. Something was up. She pressed the button to raise the bed upright. The nurse's aide had left the sides down after her sponge bath that afternoon, so she dragged one leg over the side, then the other. She sat on the edge to let the dizziness subside, then carefully plotted her path so she wouldn't yank out any wires or tubing, not wanting to set off any alarms. Jeanette would not be happy. She took her mask off and tested the air. There was no air and she put it back on. The clear tube was long enough to get to the chair by the window. Grabbing the metal tree that held bags of fluids, she slowly, excruciatingly, shuffled the three feet to the chair and flopped down on it, gasping. The crows were gathered in the cottonwoods, their attention on the double utility doors, and rats were leaping out of the dumpster. Garbage must be coming. Dinner. Someone in a black bomber jacket came out and set all the crows to cawing at once, but he wasn't carrying a bag. He didn't even go to the dumpster, but walked over to the white refrigerated trailer instead and unlocked it. When he turned to open the door she could read the back of his jacket. Boulder Coroner. He waved to someone inside the hospital, and two women wheeled a gurney out. They wore the same bomber jacket, like a sports team. The Boulder Coroners. Their slogan, Nature always bats last. On the gurney was a white plastic bag, and the crows went berserk. The three coroners quickly maneuvered the body into the trailer, and when they stepped out, one of the women looked up at the hospital and seemed to sigh.

What had Shelley thought was in there? Had she never wondered? The women wheeled the empty gurney back into the hospital while the man stood guard at the trailer and they rolled out another body bag, and then another. The crows settled. Finally the man closed the trailer door and locked it, and the team went back in the hospital and the double doors closed behind them. One by one the birds raised their wings and floated down to the dumpster.

Alpenglow radiated pink behind the mountains and she yearned to be walking the foothills to be awash in that healing light, to be so high up she could turn around and view her life at a distance. She wondered if she could locate that trail again after all this time. She wanted to find the spot where the deer had been and collect the weathered bones in a pile, then top it with the skull. She wanted to sit and wait for the mountain lion who'd killed it, who surely watched her every move and knew exactly where she was. There was a lightness in her chest and she felt herself glowing with love for them both. She wanted to grab them together and hug them, like they were family.

She really needed to lie down. She had to get back to the bed but she wasn't sure how. She'd used up all her strength and the call button was out of reach. She should just stay where she was and wait, but she had to lie down, now. She could do this, she thought. She'd done it before.

Shelley did not know how she ended up on the ground. She did not remember falling. Jeanette ran in and said "What the hell," and called for help on the intercom. Shelley's mask must have slipped off because she couldn't seem to breathe. More nurses in protective gear arrived and surrounded her. One nurse pushed the chair out of the way and glanced out the window. "I hear they have to bring in another trailer."

"Don't be looking out there," said Jeanette. "Get me the paddles."

Shelley didn't know what the rush was. She wasn't in any pain, although she sensed her body wasn't arranged quite right. Maybe her wings were in the way. She heard a long shrilling sound.

"Oh, the hawk," she thought. "The hawk is here."

Good Job, Robin

AHIMSA CUPPED HER hands and waved an elbow. "Isaura! Look!" She had to shout to be heard over my earplugs, and for a moment I panicked thinking she was feeling woozy again. But no, she just had something she wanted to show me. I leaned over the sorting table to look, and with a smile she opened her tawny hands like a flower, just enough so I could peek inside. Two stamens wiggled in the darkness.

No, not stamens. Antennae. I took my plugs out. "It's just a cricket, Ahimsa. One of a billion crickets under this dome, every one of them chirping like an insect possessed."

"Isaura," she sighed. "First of all, not *all* of them are chirping, only males do that. Second, *look*. He's not one of many." With that, the flower bloomed again, revealing a dark, armored head. Okay, then. I set aside my preconceived notion of "cricket" so that I could see this particular one. It was part of our general training, but of course, Ahimsa was so much better at it than I was. I examined his (no female ovipositor) powerful legs and striated wings, counted two feathered arms, then looked him in the eye.

"Purple eyes?"

"Purplish. That's what I'll call him. I want to set him free later."

The farm collaborative did not discourage random release. Talos would want a genoscan, but after that, the crickets were sterile so there was no danger of wiping out any precarious ecosystem. Purplish would also go through sensors with us when we left to check for paralysis virus, a hazard not just for farmed crickets, but for the small rewilded populations. The collaborative only asked that if you took a cricket you took care. No cruelty. If you wanted to eat it, fine, but be merciful and quick. No eating it alive. If you wanted to release it, be responsible about freedom. Find an environment with a steady supply of food, and make sure other crickets were around. Loneliness was its own cruelty.

"Lucky guy," I said, putting my plugs back in.

Ahimsa and I were working at a cricket farm for our Nourishment requirement, part of our Global Service exploring how food connects us to the earth. After the Extinction Emergency of the early millennium, it didn't take long for even the thickest human to realize that if our species was going to survive—and that is still not a given—we could no longer view nature as a commodity to be exploited. Our self-anointed place in the web of life was total apex and in our greed we nearly devoured the planet. Now we had to turn it around, although there were those, like Ahimsa, who believed the best way to heal the earth was for us to leave it, and the way she eats, she's halfway there.

In her defense, learning to feed ourselves without wide-scale defaunation or adding to the methane load is a challenge. Crickets are a fair option. They're fed vegetable waste, are high in protein, and what little gas they release is captured and used in the running of the farm. But dear Jiminy, the noise. I hadn't thought that part all the way through. The males could be bred without the ability to chirp, but the Ethics Board ruled that their lives would be diminished without their song. And so we let crickets be crickets and I stop up my ears.

Ahimsa flapped her elbow at me again and I took the earplugs out. Again. "I don't understand why we raise them only to kill them," she said, wrangling Purplish into a carrier the size of her fist. "If they're going to be eaten, why give them life?"

I like to eat crickets whole as nature intended, like a crunchy snack, but most people eat them dehydrated and ground into meal, not wanting to find a leg or mandible. Some folks are revolted at the thought of eating bugs in any form, but not me. Humans are food generalists. Disgust might help us avoid pathogens but if you can get past that, insects greatly expand options and survivability. Whatever it takes is my motto. Animal-sourced nutrition is a constant debate, not just between me and Ahimsa, but throughout the

Zones. "Corpse food," she calls it. I just call it dinner.

There is no farming of mammals for food, but some of us in the Lower UK Zone eat rewilded deer and rabbits, whose fertility has proved robust. Unlike many creatures, they are successfully breeding on their own, still passing on the original genetic adjustments Talos designed for them soon after the Emergency. But without predators to keep these populations in check they'll strip the land bald in no time, so until we can bring back lynx and wolves, humans must intervene. Harvesting is done by hunting, a food-gathering activity that meets Ethics Board guidelines for the respectful treatment of animals. They get to lead free lives in the wild before a swift and unsuspecting end. "Better death on the fly than the abattoir," as my old man used to say. "We should all be so lucky." He took me hunting when I was young, but that ended when he did. It would have ended when I married Ahimsa anyway, although when hunt meat is offered, I jump on it, no matter how she carries on. It's considered sacred to those of us who partake. Sometimes I can feel the creature's wild heart beating in my own.

Ahimsa gently touched the cricket's head and it lunged at her. Crickets were feisty, if not downright violent, but the Ethics Board kept them the way they were. Go figure. "He's got such spirit," she said as she closed the carrier. "I just don't understand."

"Ahimsa," I said, "you know the answer. Life needs life." All sorts of living tissue was biofabricated in labs, but the process still relied on plant or animal cells to begin with. Not even Talos can make food out of stone. Ahimsa feels strongly about taking life, even plant life, and is one of those who eats only fallen fruit or vegetables. In other words, vegetable waste, just like our crickets. Talos tries to meet those needs, but that sort of diet depends on the continuous availability of fallen foods, and since nothing is continuously available it's not encouraged. In my opinion, it doesn't embrace a particularly healthy grasp of our dietary impulses either. I tell her, only decomposers like worms and pill bugs wait for dinner to land on the dirt.

"I wish we'd gotten placed at a butterfly farm," she said, as she picked up her sorting wand, separating mature crickets from the others at their feeding station.

"Me too." Magical was how those places were described. The butterfly's role in the food web was not as an edible but pollinator, and in areas that can't support sufficient plant life, nectar stations were installed so butterflies can be released simply for our joy. The same with fireflies. Not like ants, who seemed to be released for our annoyance. We started out at the ant farm, raising them for soil restoration as well as food. They'd hide in our turbans, hitching rides back to our community dome where they took over the kitchen. They died out eventually because, like farmed crickets, they are sterile. Even if they weren't already bred that way, it's unlikely they could produce anything that resembled an "ant" on their own.

During the Emergency, hot soil forced them out into the open, making their DNA as damaged as ours. We, like many other organisms, still have to be genetically assisted to tolerate radiation, toxins, and lower oxygen levels. There was an uproar about it at first, but honestly, we were going down fast and it was best to hand regeneration over to artificial intelligence systems like Talos. Nothing could have survived without its genetic guidance. Nothing. Well, except maybe cockroaches and rats, who seemed to have come through even stronger. We should all have those genes. We probably do. Talos really knows how to mine the universal code to get us where we are today: Still alive.

As I inserted my plugs back in yet again, I snuck a look at Ahimsa. She was so fragile she could be sucked up in an exhaust fan, but at the moment she seemed well enough. She was whistling along with the crickets as she swept them into their trays. No earplugs for her. She was prone to existential jitters, so her medic told her to immerse herself in the task at hand to keep from fretting about the world. Ha.

Adapting humans to toxins and the degraded atmosphere has been a success, but the Ethics Board is committed to keeping a short leash on other adjustments. They want to be able to undo any changes as we continue to reverse the earth's damage. We know what has to be done and we have the systems in place to do it. Right off, ego and politics were removed from everyday decision-making by assigning governance to Talos. Our life spans are so short our minds can't visualize long-term changes in the environment. We're not equipped, but Talos is, who selects Ethics Board members for their clear vision and righteous justice. I'm proud that a forbearer was one of these, a prominent voice in the first skin pigmentation decision. In those early Emergency generations, people died from radiation burns and those who survived could not leave shelter. A gene was modified to add a subtle metallic olive-green sheen to human skin, which reflects damaging ultraviolet rays and gave us freedom. Plus, it looks fantastic, no matter what color your base coat is. Lungs and blood have been tweaked over time, but Talos tries not to tamper with human nature, as much as I wish it would. One day we're building opera houses, the next day, gas chambers. Instead of a genetic solution, Talos developed education systems meant to instill a sense of justice, wonder, and compassion. It's a work in progress.

Team members, swaying in their colorful tunics at their tables, started humming or whistling along with Ahimsa, as if the dome wasn't loud enough. I adjusted my plugs, even though it's nice to see people content in their work. I just wish they'd keep it down.

After the Emergency, the earth was divided into thousands of Zones, each with its own Ethics Board, Talos, and Administrators. In the same way we learn a universal language while keeping our ancestral tongue, every Talos is programmed locally but uses a single code to coordinate global efforts. We have to work together or die together, as the Ethics Board reminds us. Administrators, guided by Talos, balance resources for all living things in their Zone, both plant and animal, down to the little amoeba who doesn't know what it is. We vote for new Administrators every two years, based on programmed criteria for fairness, responsibility, and diversity from a pool of candidates selected by Talos.

"Hey!" Ahimsa nudged me with her wand to get my attention. "Wake up," she said. "These have to be…" but could not finish the sentence. She handed me a covered tray of crickets to be scanned for nutritional anomalies and gene mutations. That was the big lesson learned from the Emergency: Gather the building blocks of life and preserve them deep within the lava caves of the Moon, protected from radiation. Talos continues to scrape dust from specimen drawers across the world, and all organisms are constantly sampled for any lost wetware of life, from the highest peak to the deepest sea. The MoonArk is a massive undertaking, but with it we have the raw materials for genetic rescue, and when the time is right we can bring back more species in their original configurations. But that is a decision for the Board. When I was little, I asked my mother why couldn't we have giraffes again, a fantastic long-necked creature I'd seen in a holograph show. "Just because we can do it, doesn't mean we should," she'd said. "We have to restore their environments first. We can't bring them back only to keep them imprisoned, can we

Isaura?" I shook my head no, but I really wanted a giraffe. I still do.

I finished scanning and ran the tray through the flash unit, where the crickets were instantly euthanized. I liked to spare Ahimsa that part. When this cycle is over we're applying for the plankton beds, and I'm hoping she won't start empathizing with the single-celled creatures. Petroleum started out as plankton that sank to the bottom of ancient seas, making the atmosphere safe for multi-cellular land mammals. Then a few eons later one of those mammals (us) began to extract it and burn it for energy, releasing all that carbon back into the air and making it unsafe again. We knew what the science was and did it anyway. That's humans in a nutshell. Out at sea, we'll be raising plankton on floating beds to absorb carbon from the atmosphere, then, as they sink in death they'll take the carbon with them, reversing the fossil fuel process. We'll also learn to cultivate it for food, fertilizer, fuel, and biomaterials, the first products to replace the original oil-based plastics. What a difference that's made in restoring the oceans. Except for jellyfish (makes a nice soup) we harvest no sea animal for food yet. In the meantime, we, even Ahimsa, dine on algae and seaweed in dozens of different forms, although she'll only eat them if they've washed up on shore.

This sensitivity of hers didn't bode well for the Mass Mortality Events of our Global Service. Everyone has to work three months at a land or water MME site to document places where species, including our own, died en masse from oxygen deprivation or some other hideous end. We'll gather bones and collect soil samples. We'll bear witness. Most MMEs were preventable, but no one acted to prevent them. We thought only of what we wanted and how to get it. Now, from birth, we're encouraged to think about the ways we're connected to other living things. But some people, like Ahimsa, hardly need more training and I worry that her body will crumble like dust.

Still, it'll be fun to live on the ocean. We want to experience as much as we can before we decide on our life's work and settle down to start a family. Humans could be generated by laboratory systems like other species, but that is absolutely, positively not allowed by the Board. Natural humans are difficult enough without lab humans running around. And yet, until Talos can clean up lingering genetic horrors, natural insemination, even when possible, is still frowned upon. Talos screens out mutations before fertilization takes place and it's all in vitro from there. Ahimsa wants children but only if the earth wants them. Talos calculates the number of humans that can be supported on the planet every year, which is far below what it was at Peak Human over two centuries ago, but enough to make us feel established again, if somewhat sparse in most places. Ahimsa believes that one year Talos will come to the conclusion that keeping our species around isn't worth it anymore, and will put an end to our regeneration. I told her that's not possible, that Talos is programmed

Too much world-building. When does the story start?

to incorporate us back into a balanced ecosystem. "It should be programmed for the planet to survive, with or without us," she said.

"Let's just let Talos do its job," I said. At any rate, if Ahimsa ever overcomes her hesitancy, we'll use sperm cells made from our bone marrow so we can fertilize each other's eggs. Ahimsa wants to carry them both, even though she could not possibly support a pregnancy if she doesn't start eating for one, never mind for two.

Same-sex couple or everyone both?

The farm clock chimed in with the crickets and Ahimsa motioned with her carrier to say, "Let's go." We have one last chore, and it's the best. At the end of each day, workers take crates of live crickets outside the city to distribute in fields as prey for rewilded birds and toads. Birds, especially, need a consistent food supply or they'll fly off, a survival mechanism Talos is having trouble controlling. If they migrate to where insects and seed-bearing plants have not been re-established they'll perish.

We loaded our crates into a chartreuse transport at the dock, a sweet ride that hovers centimeters above the ground and flies like an earth-hugging hawk. As we strapped ourselves into the cab, Ahimsa put the cricket container between us. "Should we let him go in the field with the others?" I asked, pressing a button to send us to a location preprogrammed by Talos.

"No, I want to give him a better chance than that," said Ahimsa. "I want to release him near us, in the pollination field at Cathedral Park."

I didn't point out that he would have predators in town as well. Not so many birds and certainly no toads, but wow, the rats. Even I won't eat rat, in spite of their abundance. The vermin-coded cats keep disappearing (hopefully as animal companions and not food), so until the labs catch up with predator production, Purplish was no safer in a city park.

Purplish was quiet in his carrier, but the other crickets chirped like rowdy teens going to a concert. When we arrived at our field, we opened the crates and they leaped out in sprays of joy. Because the atmosphere outside the city is not always stable, we wore safety hoods over our turbans and took an occasional puff from our oxygen. Humans evolved to be outdoors, so Talos designed systems to make that possible. One day soon, we're assured, we can rely solely on natural air. A restored ozone will even allow us to grow hair again.

Ahimsa was a little shaky on her feet, so we went back to our transport with the empty crates to watch the crickets disperse. They were exuberant, taking thrilling leaps and climbing up grass stalks that swayed under their weight, like they were born there. It wasn't long before a flash of ruddy-orange came swooping down and carried off a kicking cricket.

"Good job, robin," I said.

"Why do you say that? It's so annoying."

"I say it because the bird is doing what it's supposed to do. Eat."

"But it's eating another living thing. Why can't it just eat seed

Story is too didactic, Shoehorned exposition.

on the ground?" Ahimsa sighed. "Why?"

"That's not its nature. We have to give each rewilded species what they need to survive. If we mess too much with the robin's nutritional needs it'll be a different bird. It might not even be a bird." Early on in the Emergency, ravens had darkened the skies and eaten all the song birds. Bringing back the robin was huge. When I hear one sing, all my brain cells light up.

"It doesn't seem fair," she said, lifting her eyeshield to wipe her tears. Her shield took up so much of her face she looked like a bug.

"No one ever said nature was fair."

"How is this even nature?" She pointed to the field, a field that had been completely engineered by Talos, down to the thinnest blade of grass.

"It's nature perfectly recreated," I said, starting up the transport. "It's this or a burnt, lifeless landscape. Take your pick. Which 'nature' do you want?"

She didn't answer and I didn't push it. What was the point? As we swung towards the city, she clutched the cricket box in her lap and looked at anything but me. It was a long ride back. We left our transport and crates at the depot outside the city and rode to the park on the hydrogen rail. Ahimsa stared out the window at the passing domes. When our Nourishment section ends we'll move on to Shelter. For safety's sake, the trend has been to build down then cap it with a filter dome, but we've asked to work with the tissue technology division to grow living homes, a tree-like network connected by roots. She pointed at a budding oak, planted in the Great Reforestation. "Wouldn't you like to live in a tree?"

"Can we keep the squirrels out?" I asked, which for some reason made her laugh, and I was relieved. It was good to see her happy. I took her hand and she squeezed it, and we explored my complicated feelings about squirrels for the rest of the ride. From the hub we walked into city center down pebbled lanes full of workers jostling towards the end of their day, and night workers just starting theirs. As we rounded the corner to the park, we came upon an emotional health crisis. A young man was crouched on the ground, wearing a dirty white tunic and sobbing uncontrollably. His turban had slipped off, exposing a scalp that was scratched raw. A health team knelt by his side and spoke to him in whispers as the crowd parted like water and gave them space. We were quiet the rest of the way, and I could feel Ahimsa slipping off to her dark place again. I was not surprised that when we got to the park, she wasn't ready to let go of Purplish. "Maybe he'd be happier living with us in the dome?" she asked.

"You think so?" I asked, knowing he would not be. Knowing she knew he would not be. To buy some time for her to make the right decision, I steered us to a food-kiosk to pick up dinner. Shaped like giant mushrooms, the bright red kiosks were plentiful and evenly distributed around the city, with prepared food or groceries supplied by central underground kitchens. No one went hungry unless they tried. I looked at Ahmisa.

"How about a cricket wrap for me and a high-tide algae burger for you?"

funny

"You wouldn't eat cricket today, would you?" She held the carrier to her chest like I was going to pounce on it.

"I like cricket wraps. And they're good for you. Amino acids, iron, B vitamins. I wish you'd try one. I'm not sure you're getting all the B you need."

"If crickets have all that maybe they also have consciousness," said Ahimsa. "And a soul."

"I don't doubt they have consciousness," I said. "They might even have a soul. But we have to eat something."

"Do we?" she asked.

"Yes. We do. We all have to do our part to stay alive if any of us are going to survive. It might even be our obligation."

"If we're all so connected, then everything we eat is just cannibalism."

me

"Stop that. Just stop it!"

She stared at me in shock, her mouth a twisted line. I was a little surprised myself, but my anger came from a swirling well of fear. She was getting more extreme, even scary, and when she turned and ran into the park I was glad to see her go.

I sensed people on the street staring at me, so I pulled myself together. Breathe in, breathe out. Focus on the task at hand. Dinner. Maybe not cricket today, after all. I tapped on the pictograph of a lab-generated wrap produced from plant cells and lamb genes, then scanned my hand. The roll-up soon appeared in a kiosk window, warm and ready to go. Ahimsa could figure out what, or if, she wanted to eat, but I was done arguing about it. If she really believed that eating in itself was cannibalism, there was no hope. Granted, cannibalism had been a real blight on the human legacy, but those years were behind us and had no bearing on me eating culled deer or dining on the complex feat of food engineering I held in my hands. Interconnectedness did not mean the "same as."

I looked around for the young man in crisis. He was up and walking now, moving slowly, painstakingly slowly, towards the re-health center, supported by the team. Ahimsa would not be far behind him the way she was going. Hunger was her virtue now. I wasn't ready to go after her, but I also wasn't going to let her keep me from going to Cathedral Park on my own. It was a rejuvenating place to be, surrounded by mechanical carbon-pumps and filled with nature's pumps, the trees. As I entered the park, I turned off my oxygen pack and took a quick glance over at the pollination field. No Ahmisa, and that was fine with me. I found an empty bench and ate my wrap alone, chewing in thought. I watched children toss a violet ball in a circle from one to another, laughing, choosing to play and be happy. Was that our real nature, before the problems

Overall seems not at her usual level.

of the world had their way with us? I know we are a little sad right now. We've suffered a great deal these last generations. Our ancestors died young, making us tentative and wary. We know our place in the world is even less important than plankton, but still, we've worked hard to restore what we've destroyed. We're getting tired, but we have to believe that the worst is behind us.

I breathed in the real air, filling my lungs with it. Of course, as our educators keep reminding us, in the same way nourishment was more than food, survival was more than just breathing. We must find a way to thrive. We must find joy and meaning in life. But how? What did meaning even mean? Or life for that matter? If atoms were made from energy, and everything was made from atoms, then how do we even stand up? Talos doesn't have those answers, nor does it think we need to know to get on with it, but it encourages metaphysical exploration through spiritual practice and the arts. Sometimes Ahimsa and I go to the clay yards to create wild, sinuous sculptures that look like giant slugs, which we leave in the fields and woods. It helps us feel connected to the flow of earth's energy, and maybe the answer is as simple as that.

I ate my delicious wrap and watched the shadows of the Cathedral's gothic spires lengthen in the field. These old buildings have been retooled as Numinous Heritage Sites, where holy ones and scholars gather to study the ancient texts index, working with the Ethics Board as needed. There are no organized religions as such, but most of us hold beliefs of some variation of paganism with a splash of quantum theory. Both are all about the energy. In that spirit, the cathedral doors are as open as loving arms. Ahimsa and I got married here. A holy one, cloaked in flowing white and magenta, took our hands in theirs. "When this foundation was laid a thousand years ago," they began, "the workers knew they would never see it finished. They didn't even know how the roof would be supported, but they began their great project anyway and prayed the technology would come. I want you two to have faith in the future, and trust that the flying buttresses are on their way."

At the end of the ceremony, standing under the vaulted ceiling and the magnificent stained glass, we fed each other wedding cake. The religious group that built the cathedral might have been manipulative and authoritarian, and had certainly failed to guess how the divine wanted to be worshipped, but the structure gave us faith, not in some abstract god, but in us.

Now Ahimsa was losing faith not only in us the couple, but us the species. I stood up and found a suction bin for my trash, then went to look for her. I'd promise to swear off cricket if she came with me to the clay yards that night. I headed for the cathedral steps, where people gathered in the evenings to watch the setting sun. That was one thing a degraded atmosphere had given us, wild sunsets that sparked green and purple rays from the refraction of foreign particles in the air. Talos was working to replace contaminants with protective aerosols and get us back to basic orange and red.

I saw her sitting on the top step, not looking west with the others, but looking down at Purplish, crying. The container was open as if set in her lap to catch her tears. I sat down next to her and she inched away. Lower on the steps in front of us was a small family. The parents sat on either side of a toddler, cute as a little bee in his yellow-striped tunic. They were taking turns feeding him. He was playing with a doll in his lap, but when they offered a bite of their dinner, he opened his rosebud mouth and took it, then when back to playing. "Good job," I said, not meaning to say it out loud.

"What was that?" Ahimsa snapped.

"Cute," I said, pointing to the toddler.

She looked at the family and shrugged. "What's the point of children if they're just going to be endlings?"

"You don't know that. Look at them, feeding themselves so they can feed others. If you don't eat, you'll die, and then you won't be any help at all."

"I can help by dying."

I took a calming breath. Then another. "That could happen sooner than you think. It could happen without warning. And if it happens I won't survive it."

"Well, maybe none of us deserves to survive."

"You do," I told her. "I do. But we have to make difficult feeding decisions every day to survive. You have to eat or die. There's no

Cinematic

other option. I won't stay and watch you starve yourself to death."

"No one's asking you to stay," she said, then looked back down at Purplish. "Oh no!" She shook the container. "He's gone!"

"I'm sure he's right here," I said, not really believing it. We stood and moved with care so we didn't step on him, then began to search the stone steps. If this cricket thing ended poorly it could be her end too. "Maybe he hopped down to the field on his own."

"He doesn't even know what a field is," she said, choking up. "What if he wanders into a hot spot and dies?" She was having trouble breathing and I readied my pack. Others got up to help, gently shaking out their tunics and looking on the ground. Everyone knew what it was to lose something precious.

"Here! Here!" It was the toddler's father. "Inside!"

We all gathered at the carved oak and iron doors of the cathedral and stood at the threshold. This building should have crumbled long ago, and yet it continued to stand and even adapt. In the two years since we'd gotten married, the arched side aisles had been fitted with massive tubs of flowers, vegetables, and even saplings, flourishing under hidden grow panels. At the far end of the nave, full-grown trees had replaced the altar in the sanctuary.

"Listen," the mother said to her child, touching her ear. I heard a soft, resounding chirp, then another. Soon there was a chorus of them, echoing off the thick stone walls. "Cricket," she said to her son.

"Crik-ket," he repeated. "Crik-ket! Crik-ket!"

For all my complaining about chirping at the farm, I'd forgotten how rare it was to hear it out in the world. Chirping was the very pulse of nature. Native field crickets had been an early casualty of the Emergency and here we were, bringing them back. Their sizes were mixed so it seemed to be a true rewilded population and not just a collection of sterile farm crickets. That was progress. An unexpected environment perhaps, but progress. The late afternoon sunlight poured in through the clerestory high up in the nave, sending dust-filled shafts across a space so staggeringly tall it could have been designed by giraffes. Ahimsa pointed at Purplish on the floor a few meters away, where he blended in with the mottled tiles. Humans had huddled together for safety here since the 13th century, during plagues and invasions and the worst years of the Emergency. Now look. Trees and crickets. Purplish twitched his antennae and rubbed his wings together, creating his song. "Chirup-chirup-chirup." He continued to inch his way towards his species who were waiting for him among the flowers and plants. And then he began to eat.

"If you say 'good job' I'm going to scream," said Ahimsa, but she said it with a begrudging smile.

I took her hand and she did not yank it away. "I was actually going to say Lucky Guy. Because of you."

She shook her head. "In spite of me. He chose his own safe place." She paused. "But you're right about the kid. I guess he's pretty cute."

"I'll bet he'd love to see a giraffe. But if we're not here, we can't bring them back. You need to start eating harvested plant material as well as the fallen."

She considered Purplish munching on a living leaf and did not answer. I walked over to the grow tub and picked a green pod from a leafy vine and brought it back to her. I ran my thumbnail along the seam revealing a row of pale beans lying on their velvety case like cosseted babies. She plucked one from the line-up, holding the bean in two fingers and stared at it. I pried one from the pod and held it up to her. I saw the struggle in her eyes, and then I saw the surrender. She opened her mouth and I placed the bean gently on her tongue. With a little hesitation she drew it in, chewed a bit, then swallowed. She nodded. She could do this. She held her bean up and I opened my mouth.

Float

GOD HELP US.

The words, writ large in the sand, appeared on the beach after Duncan Leland's attention had already drifted. It was in the pink of the afternoon, at the end of another trying day, when he should have been attempting something spectacularly proactive to save his sinking business, such as scrambling numbers on a screen or gathering somber consultants around him, but instead, as was his habit, he was looking for answers outside his office window. The sky was clear and blue, the water calm. The serenity of the day mocked the economic storm raging around him. He was now, as Harvey Storer of Coastal Bank & Trust had so coldly pointed out to him that morning, officially underwater. He owed more on Seacrest's Ocean Products of Maine, Ltd. than the business was worth.

"True that," Duncan had agreed, "but only at this very moment."

"What else is there?" asked Storer.

A leveling silence washed over Duncan as his mind slowly

emptied of words. He was opening and shutting his mouth like a fish when Storer, sitting across from him at the loan desk, leaned in closer.

"Duncan? What else do you have that might secure this loan?"

Duncan shook himself out of his trance, realizing that Storer's was a fiscal rather than a philosophical challenge. "It's all here," he said, half-standing as he slapped pages of the loan application down on the mahogany like tarot cards. "Look, in the spring, our new line of fertilizer hits the market, opening a revenue stream so robust it'll be like drinking water from a firehose!" He displayed a spreadsheet thick with projections, but this banker, like the ones who came before him, remained unmoved. Duncan's vision of rosy profits in the future failed to overcome the devalued assets of the present, and in that moment he saw his business begin to slide away.

He'd left Storer's sterile cubicle in a funk and gone back to his office, back to the warm embrace of his chair and the tranquilizing effect of the harbor view. He fixed his gaze on the beach, a patch of rust-streaked sand so inhospitable it did not even exist at high tide, and let his mind fix on a plastic bag caught on a submerged stick. He watched the bag, alive with water, wash gently from side to side until his own currents of thought slowed to a listless tempo. After an empty space of time, the retreating tide abandoned both stick and bag to the land and his hypnotic amusement was over. Looking back, he was sure of one thing. There had been no one on the beach and there had been no mysterious message written in the sand. That was two things, but still.

He wondered, sometimes, if he might have been a witness to the event if the music hadn't ended. He liked to keep an iPod playing on the factory floor, on the theory that if he was asking his employees to spend their days cooking fish skeletons down to a fine powder, then he had better give them some background music to divert their senses. If nothing else, managing the sound system was one of the few enjoyable duties left to him, so when a cycle of early Beatles ended, he turned his back on the water view to deliberate at length between Playlist #8 (Miles, Coltrane, and Rufus Harley) and Playlist #22 (Dylan, Joni, and Steve Earle) before abandoning hope of coming to any decision at all. He clicked Shuffle in defeat and returned to his chair. When he looked back down at the beach, there, scratched into the sand, were the three-foot high wobbly letters spelling out *God Help Us*. The surface was still reflective from its recent brush with water. The message faced the harbor, not him, so it didn't appear to be a personal accusation, more like a random act of prayer. Or not. Worst case scenario, it was written by an employee petitioning God on behalf of Seacrest's. But no matter who wrote it or what the intention was, it was a desperate message and a bad one for potential investors, should he ever have any. It had to go.

Down, down to the sea he climbed, taking the two iron flights of the fire escape to avoid his factory workers, who seemed to want so much from him these days, most of all an optimistic face on Seacrest's future. Gone, gone, gone. It was low tide now and his heels sank into the wet sand as he trudged towards the words, his footprints filling with water behind him. With the tip of his black rubber boot, he proceeded to rub out the message, erasing the *d* first, changing *God Help Us* to *Go Help Us*.

"Better," he mumbled. More ecumenical, more in keeping with his Unitarian ancestry. Then he contemplated *Us*, that sweet plural pronoun of marriage. He rubbed it out. It was the middle of August when Cora asked for a little air and here it was after Labor Day and he still hadn't heard back from her whether she'd caught her breath. He stood very still, trying to quell the sour tide in his gut. How had the solid continent of *Us* become the scattered islands of *him* and *her?* They had just wanted what everyone else seemed to have. "Is a baby really too much to ask for?" as Cora would say. "They're everywhere!"

He should have known that to have expectations was to court disappointment. Two years ago they'd decided it was time to add to their fund of general happiness, but nature had not taken its usual course in the bedroom. Was it her? Was it him? Or were they just a bad combination? But Cora, even-keeled as she was, wouldn't let them go there. "No finger pointing," she'd said, "let's just get the problem solved," and in July they began to take deliberate steps towards in vitro. At the very first appointment, he was asked for a sperm sample to test for motility. He found the staff oddly humorless about the situation and his jokes fell flat, but he got the job done. Afterwards, it was he who fell flat. He froze in the hallway with the filled specimen cup in hand, locked in terror as if staring into a milky abyss. A nurse had to wrest the container from him, and from then on his marriage began to spiral down the drain.

The problem was this: Fertility treatment had led him to think about the dangers of replicating his family's genes, and those worries began to bloom like algae in a stagnant pond. The next thing he knew he was debating whether it was right to bring children into the world at all, a world so overcrowded and polluted it sat on the brink of ecological extinction. This, in turn, led to questions about the meaning of life itself. "When we give them life, we give them death," he said. "What's the point?"

That was it for Cora. "Enough thinking," she'd said through her tears, "it's time to act." Off to counseling they went, but they could not reach the line of salvage in that desolate terrain, with its boxes of tissues and anatomically correct dolls stored in a milk crate in the corner. Cora was particularly teary because she'd been getting estrogen shots in preparation for the egg harvest. Marriage counseling ended when he failed to follow through on scheduling an appointment, a chore the therapist insisted they take turns doing, a tactic which seemed like some kind of test. He remembered the moment he stalled out. He had been, as was his habit, gazing out of his office window, watching the Hood Dairy blimp hover in the air above a distant beach. *Enjoy Hood Ice Cream* was printed on the rounded sides, sending him into a smiling reverie of dripping vanilla cones, sand buckets and other childhood joys. "Enjoy it *all*," he'd said out loud. He continued to watch until the blimp turned inland, but instead of majestically disappearing over the horizon as usual, it slowly—ever, ever so slowly—dipped too close to the tree-tops. The navigation bucket got stuck in the branches and it could not move. Engine trouble, he'd found out later. No one was hurt, but how could he make an appointment after that?

"What kind of a world is this where a zeppelin can just fall out of the sky?" he said to Cora. It was the day when he'd gone to Portland to produce the specimen for the first attempt at implantation later that week, so he was particularly shook up. "How can we bring a child into a world that hasn't even mastered 19th century technology?"

Cora was as unmoved as the zeppelin. "Fuck the blimp," she said. She was a family therapist herself, and as far as she was concerned his inability to make the appointment demonstrated not just his lack of commitment to the process, but a lack of commitment to her and their future baby. Like a cruise ship, Cora was not easy to turn around once she was set on a particular heading. She started throwing ballast overboard. She sent Duncan away that very night.

"Go to Slocum's for a few days to get your head on straight. You're too anxious to be around right now."

Their relationship had been sitting in dead air ever since. But that was not today's problem. His marriage would have to wait in a long line of tomorrow's problems, because today he had to save his business. Seacrest's was letting in water at every seam and it was all his fault. He had aimed too high. He should have opted for the cheapest solution he could get away with two years ago when the EPA mandated the installation of pollution controls, but no, in the spirit of the careless prosperity of the times, he'd wandered off to where the woodbine twineth and borrowed too much money for a complete modernization of the plant, making it as clean and tight as a toolbox. The banks were crazy to loan him so much money. How much profit, really, could be had from fish waste? Seacrest's, whose business was to process marine waste into feed and fertilizer, used to be known, along with all the other gurry or dehydration plants on the coast, as the smelly stepchild of Maine's fishing world. Now the renovated plant was almost odorless. The industry had come a long way since his great-great-grandfather Lucius Leland's time, when gurry—the finny bones and entrails leftover from cleaning the day's catch—was unceremoniously dumped into the harbor, only to wash up on shore later in the day. Lucius was originally from bustling New Bedford, but he dropped anchor in Port Ellery in the name of love for a local lass and soon saw wealth where others saw garbage. Using the money he'd raised touring the Midwest with a sawdust-stuffed whale in a boxcar, he built a factory to dry and grind up the fish scraps for livestock feed. The first thing he processed was his whale. The pet food industry soon became a major buyer as well and business boomed for over a century, but in the last few decades they'd had to branch out just to keep up. His father developed their unique fish fertilizer, and more recently Duncan had added kelp to the recipe after watching Cora gather seaweed from the beach for her garden.

Kelp. He looked at *Go Help*, then changed the *H* in *Help* to a *K* and added an exclamation point.

"*Go Kelp!*" he shouted, then looked around but there was no one to hear. Not even the gang of seagulls patrolling the water's edge had paused to consider his outburst. As was too often the case these days, his words only made sense to him. *Go Kelp!* could be the name of his new retail line of soil amendments, if there was a future for them at all. Before the expensive renovations to the building, he'd always sold his fertilizer in barrels to companies who resold the powder in small bags under their own pricey labels, but as the bills came flooding in, some daft accountant said that the only way to recoup his capital expenditure was to leave the safe harbor of wholesale and set out into the deep waters of retail. Which meant more money out the door. His marketing investment had been huge and the product was still not launched. Worse, competition was darkening the sky. A dehyde down in Massachusetts had contracted with key fish processors for their waste and was already selling eco-sludge directly to the planting public. Another company in northern Maine was peddling lobster shell dust and getting as much play in the gardening magazines as a dazzling new rose. He hadn't acted fast enough in making the transition. The words he'd overheard in a bar ten years ago, soon after he took his father's place at Seacrest's, came back to him now: "Duncan Leland run a business? He couldn't run a bath."

One of the seagulls bounced closer with an eye towards a blue shell near his foot. Duncan kicked the mussel to the bird so it could see for itself that it was empty, then with a start, he realized that there were no footprints on the beach other than his. How was that possible? Someone wrote the words without walking on the sand? He looked around, then up. He was lost in troubled thought when a ship's horn sounded, frightening the seagulls into the air with hysterical shrieks and a slow flapping of wings.

All but one. There was always one.

The large black-back gull had a loop of a six-pack holder stuck in its beak and around its neck, so that the sharp plastic dug into the sides of its face. The rest of the holder was bunched up around its head and two of the loops formed glasses through which the bird stared at him with red burning eyes. One wing hung limply by its side, dragging in the sand. The poor bastard could hardly move without making things worse and Duncan knew that feeling all too well. The kindest thing to do was to let nature take its course, but when the bird opened its beak in mute appeal Duncan realized he was screwed. He'd have to give it a fighting chance or never face his friend Josefa Gould again. Josefa ran Seagull Rescue out of her backyard, a cramped space where the birds went to linger in pain before dying. He looked up at the factory. He couldn't see anyone at the windows because of the harsh reflection of the sun. But even though he couldn't see his employees, he could feel their eyes upon him and in his mind he heard them laughing.

Let them. Wounded animals had to stick together.

He held his arms out, fluttering his hands, and as he edged slowly towards the injured gull he felt himself to be the ridiculous figure his employees thought he was. He could hear Cora telling him in the measured cadence of her profession that he was being paranoid, that he had the love and respect of all his employees. But this was not paranoia; how he wished it were. Ever since his father died, forcing Duncan to move back from New York to take over Seacrest's helm—his older brother Nod having laughed it off—he felt he was not meeting the employees' expectations of a Leland boss. Duncan had arrived at the tail end of a long line of rugged, blond male specimens who were athletic, competent, and self-assured on land and sea. He was none of those things. Baby pictures showed him as a happy towhead, but the years had darkened his hair along with his mood, until now both were mud-colored. Behind his back, he imagined that his workers made fun of his coordination (faulty) and glasses (eyes too dry for contacts). He was tall, yes, but tall in a gangly, loose-limbed sort of way. His image was not helped by the fact that at the moment he wore a business suit tucked into calf-high muck boots. After he'd returned from the bank with an empty begging bowl, he was too tired to change into his work clothes of jeans and sweatshirt. He'd removed his tie and tossed it up and over the ceiling fan like a noose, then slipped off his leather shoes and put on the wellies he kept in his office for slogging around the factory floor, but he'd done nothing to protect his navy Brooks Brothers outfit. What did it matter? He saw no future that included a three-piece suit.

Taking care not to slip on the amber blobs of jellyfish that had been stranded by the tide, Duncan feigned left and the bird bobbed right, back and forth they went, tangoing their way slowly to the crumbling seawall where the gull could be cornered among the debris. If the harbor of Port Ellery, Maine, was anatomical, they now stood firmly in the appendix. The town, all red-brick and shadows, was neatly centered in the groin between two intertwining estuaries that flowed into the harbor like crossed legs. Protected coves formed armpits and piney islands spread across the skin of water like raised hives. Seacrest's sat off the harbor's irregular belly, in a small unnavigable loop prone to collecting trash. Blue rubber gloves and pieces of yellow rope were dashed twice daily against the seawall, then fell behind the dark wet rocks. Twisted metal shrines of lobster traps had dug into the beach to become part of the natural landscape, but plastic water bottles and featherweight polystyrene coffee cups were the transient and windblown accessories. Some days the tide took it all away, other days it left it all behind.

The gull's options narrowed and it turned its back to the wall, preparing to hold its ground. Duncan removed his jacket and held it aside like a toreador. The air blowing in off the harbor was cool but the warmth of the sun on his back reminded him it was still technically summer. "It's not over yet," he said to the bird and moved carefully towards it, attempting a graceful drop of the jacket, but that required him to get so close that the gull was able to slash the tender part of his palm with the curved tip of his beak before trundling away.

"Damn!" Duncan squeezed his hand and looked up at the factory. He was sure he saw people move away. Would no one come and help him? Worse, would someone come to help and expose him as a leader who could not even catch an injured gull? It was equally unthinkable that they should see him walk away from a bad situation. He had to hurry. He took hold of his jacket and with what he considered to be a superb show of agility, pounced on the bird. There ensued a whirr of elbows and wings, and for a moment Duncan thought he'd lost him, but finally, kneeling in the wet sand with sea water seeping through the wool blend of his trousers, he managed to wrap the jacket over the bird's head. Darkness calmed it down while Duncan restrained its wings with the sleeves. He was breathing hard by the time he collapsed against a barnacled rock with the neat package of gull under his arm. "For a dying bird you've got a lot of fight left in you," he said. He readjusted his glasses, then dug around in his pants pocket for his cell phone.

"Josefa, I'm on Seacrest's beach with a gull for you—bring a cage and a band-aid."

Thirteen

Minutes

Craving oblivion?

Keep your options open. See if death is really what you're after, or just a good rest. Our gun uses a clinically-tested ray instead of a bullet, so you decide how many hours of safe, monitored "death" you need. Wake up refreshed, ready to face the world again. Reasonable rates. Completely confidential. Hygienic.

(A woman in nurse's scrubs stands behind a counter staring at a computer screen. Behind her are a number of closed doors, some with red lights, others green. A man walks in. The woman looks up and smiles.)

Hi there. What can I do for you today?

I read your ad in the paper and I was wondering. What happens... what happens if you don't set a time to undo the ray's effects?

No worries. A default wake-up revives the customer in twenty-four hours, so there's no chance of an accident.

Can you override that?

I could, but I won't. You could die.

I know.

I'm not sure you understand what we do here. Refresh, Inc.'s mission is to prevent intentional deaths, not cause them. It's an epidemic. Did you know that someone kills themselves in America every twelve minutes?

I'm surprised it's not more often. Have you any idea what it's like out there?

I know. It's bad. But we can survive it, in the same way you can survive how you're feeling right now.

Please. I'll pay you double. Cash.

No. Experience a safe suicide here, then return to your life. Tell me your name.

Sam.

Sam, I'm Bethany. Tell me. Do you have family? Children?

I suppose. Two teenage girls.

You'll devastate those kids if you commit suicide. If you can't think of yourself, think of them.

I am thinking of them. I'll be one less carbon footprint on the planet. You'd be doing a great service to everyone if you just turned off the safety mechanism and let me drift away.

No. That would be murder. Think of me if you can't think of anyone else. Think of my franchise.

I'll sign anything you want. I'll get it notarized.

Go to a state that allows it. Find a doctor.

I am a doctor.

Then what are you waiting for? Just write yourself a prescription and be done with it.

I can't. I'm afraid of throwing up. I need your help.

I'll help by giving you this number to call for depression.

I don't have depression. I have a diagnosis. A bad one. I'm just waiting to die, and I hate waiting.

I'm so sorry. Many terminally ill come here thinking they'd like to end it, but leave with a renewed purpose for the time they have left. May I ask? Cancer?

No. Human mortality.

Sam, we're all human. We're all dying. Go home and enjoy the journey.

I want an exit ramp and I want it now. (He pulls out a gun and aims it at her.) Override the refresh button.

You're kidding? You have a gun? You don't need me. Just use it on yourself.

I can't. I'm a coward.

But brave enough to shoot me? What then? You'll go to jail. They'll take your shoelaces so you can't even hang yourself. If you really think there's no hope, then go find a tall building and jump. Just leave.

I can't. I'm afraid of heights. And the pain. I don't want any pain.

A razor blade?

I faint at the sight of blood.

What kind of a doctor are you?

A psychiatrist.

Of course you are. Put that gun down, Sam, or I'll call the police.

I wonder if I can get them to shoot me.

No. You're much too white.

(Sam starts sobbing. Bethany comes around the counter, takes the gun from him, and puts it next to the computer. Then she gently guides him to a door with a green light.)

Sam, you don't want to die, you just want to stop hurting. Lie right down here. I'll give you the maximum. Twenty-four hours. This one is on me, because I like you and want you to live.

But you don't love me. No one loves me. Not even I love me.

What's important is that you have the ability to love. I think you have this giant heart and that's why you're in so much pain.

It's true. I love my girls.

Good. What else?

I used to love my ex-wife. And I've always loved carrots. I love when a flock of sparrows sit on a wire all facing one direction. How do they do that?

The world is an amazing place, isn't it? It's not all misery out there. There's also beauty and poetry. Now I want you to take this ray gun, hold it to your temple, then press the trigger. You'll hear a soothing gunshot sound, then you'll be out.

Can you do it for me? I'm afraid.

No, you have to do it yourself. Those are the rules. You have to want it bad enough.

It's bad enough. It's worse than enough.

(Lying on the gurney, staring at the ceiling, he holds the ray gun to his head and finally shoots. There is a sharp noise and the gun falls to the floor. Bethany picks it up and puts it back on the charger. She looks at her watch. Thirteen minutes from door to oblivion. Score one for the team.

She returns to the counter and picks up the real gun and stares at it. She puts it to her temple, closes her eyes, sighs and smiles.)

Organic, Local, and Cruelty-Free

EVELYN TOOK QUICK red bites of her beet salad, then pushed the plate away. The bloody color offended her. This dinner offended her. She chewed without tasting and checked her phone for the time.

Her father speared an olive with his fork from a square bowl in the center of the table. "For what amounts to a buck an olive and they can't even pit it?"

"Give it to me," said her mother. "I'll do it."

"You're supposed to be out enjoying yourself, not doing their work for them."

While her parents struggled over the olive, Evelyn picked one up with her hands and pitted it with Spartan resolution. She swallowed the briny flesh but it lodged in her throat, pressing down like a grinding stone on her heart.

"I'm starving," said Paulie, Evelyn's younger brother. He said this to the phone in his lap, fully immersed in a game with a stranger in

Indonesia. While he played, his tongue stuck out of his mouth like he was catching flies.

"We should starve on a regular basis," said her father. He ran his hand down his chest, proud of the effort he made to keep trim, religiously walking from the station to work no matter the weather. "Humans evolved in scarcity, so it's good to have our food supply cut off once in a while. It should be law! The Germans have a saying: Fattening hogs think themselves fortunate."

"We're not going to get fat in this place," said Paulie. "How long does it take to make two lousy pizzas?"

"Not lousy pizzas," said his mother. "Artisanal ones in a clay oven. They'll be here soon enough." She handed the pitted olive to her husband who left the dark, mangled fruit on his plate.

"Paulie doesn't have an 'enough' button in his brain," said Evelyn.

"Never enough for any of us," said her father, speaking in a voice meant for half the restaurant to hear. "Food is the driving force of the species. It's only when a society can count on a secure supply that it can start being civilized."

"When do we get there?" asked Evelyn.

"Get where?" her mother asked.

"Civilization. Look at us. We're going backwards." She picked up her dinner knife and slashed the air in front of her. "People aren't going to let their children starve when all the resources are squandered. We'll have to learn to fight with knives. Or else." She made a swift movement across her throat.

"Evie, please," said her mother. "We're trying to have a nice dinner out."

"College is turning you into a socialist," her father said, making an expression between a smile and a snarl that exposed his upper teeth. "I started with nothing and look where I am today. Anyone in this country can rise up if they want to. Anyone."

"The higher up you go, the more they see your butt," said Paulie. His father leaned across the table and shoved his upper arm.

"Hey," said Paulie, "you're messing with my battle."

"I wish you wouldn't play war at the table," said his mother.

"He'd better start training for combat," said Evelyn. "It's coming. And it won't be on a game app either."

"I'll be ready," said Paulie. "I'm killing the other team."

"You think that's what the next big war will be like? Us against Them on a screen?" She pressed the tip of her knife into the table. "My history professor says it won't be another country, it'll be those who have pilfered all the cake against those left without a crumb. You'll be fighting hand-to-hand with people who have nothing to lose and everything to win."

"Oh Evie," said her mother. "You tore the tablecloth." She tried to tap the threads together with her napkin, a gesture that brought Evelyn back to her childhood. Oh Evie, oh Evie. Look at what you've done. And yet it was her mother who seemed frozen in time, girlish, even as Evelyn grew up and left her behind. It made her sad against her will. She should not have come home this weekend.

"It's all wrong," she said to no one in particular. Her father's attention had turned to his drink, the mixologist's creation of the day called the Copley Fund: local apple syrup, lemon, Orleans Bitter Apple Cider Vermouth, with a Prosecco float. As he finished it off, his eyes were searching the room for the server.

"Evie," said her mother, giving up on the tablecloth and raising a bottle out of its cooler. "Have a little wine. It's your birthday."

"No. I'm allergic to sulfites."

"At least have some of this bubbly water then."

"I'm drinking tap until everyone has access to potable water."

"What?" asked her father. "Who? I have water." He lifted a glass to show her.

"Not you. The disenfranchised. People who have to drink dirty water because government has ignored the broken infrastructure where people of color live."

"Disenfranchised?" Paulie laughed without lifting his head up from his game. "They lost their McDonald's franchise?"

"Fuck you," said Evelyn.

"Evie, please," said her mother.

"Have you any idea how much we have to pay for you to go to this college of yours?" said her father. "*Any*? And all for meaningless crap. Environmental studies. What a racket."

Tears filled the hollow at the base of Evelyn's throat. The sound of the dining room intensified as voices rose above the clash of cutlery and pans and she rubbed her temples.

"How about a boyfriend?" her mother asked. "Have you met anyone nice at school?"

"Maybe she has a girlfriend," said Paulie, and Evelyn flushed.

"Don't say that," said her mother. "Evie is not a homosexual."

"Who knows?" Her father looked at Evelyn. "You should have worn a dress. You look like a dyke in those clothes."

"What if I were?" she asked. "You have to be open to love wherever you find it."

"Christ," said her father. "I don't want that sort of language at the table."

"I've got to pee," said Evelyn. She left her napkin over the remains of her salad.

Her mother called after her. "Or that language either!"

Evelyn squeezed her way past crowded tables, her eyes on the floor. She could not bear the thought of making contact with other humans. She was sick of them. She locked the bathroom door behind her and took a breath. Air. More air. She stood very still to keep the water in her body from swishing back and forth, then closed her eyes to enter her special space. A safe bright place, peopled with friends she did not know, and feelings she did not have to dissect. A new world lodged under her rib cage, spinning with joy.

Spinning, spinning. She opened her eyes and lowered herself carefully to her knees. When she lifted the toilet lid, the action itself set off stomach spasms. She flushed the toilet while she heaved unproductively a few times, then up came the beets, like pieces of heart.

There was a knock on the door. "*What?*" Evelyn snapped, assuming it was her mother.

"It's Glory, your server. Just checking you're okay."

Evelyn flushed the toilet again and opened the door a crack. Glory was not much older than she was, with a pierced lower lip and black Tweety Bird hair. One arm was thickly tattooed with tendrils and skulls and crows. She wore a blue ribbon around her neck like a Persian cat.

"I'm sorry," Glory said. "You didn't look too good going in."

"I'm all right," Evelyn said with a vague gesture towards the dining area. "It's just, my family."

"Cool. Do you need anything? Water? Food?"

"Thanks," said Evelyn. "But no. I'm not hungry."

"I live in an apartment over a funeral home so I'm always hungry. Formaldehyde is an appetite stimulant."

Evelyn laughed for the first time that night. "Then I'll have a double."

"Stick around after your family leaves and I'll buy you a drink. You can take the emergency brake off." Glory turned at the sound of her name being shouted from the kitchen. "Gotta run."

Evelyn stood at the bathroom door for a moment and looked out at the restaurant, which seemed, in the dim light, like a murky fish tank. Her mother was speaking to her inattentive family as if submerged, producing a steady stream of bubbles that rose and popped above their heads, releasing not words, but emotions. Boredom, anxiety, depression. Hunger. And in her mother she saw herself, but there was no making any of it right.

Paulie looked up from his game and stared at Evelyn with blurry eyes. His life could not be easy at home alone with her gone. She gave him a weak smile and he looked back down at his lap. She could not help him either.

"Are you okay?" her mother asked when she returned to the table.

"I am now," said Evelyn.

"What were you talking to that waitress about?" her father asked.

Before Evelyn could respond, Glory swooped in on the table with two pizzas, placing each ceremoniously on its own pedestal.

"No pepperoni?" asked Paulie, looking up from his game.

"The hell's that?" asked her father, picking at a piece of greenery on the pizza.

"Arugula," said Evelyn. "Why didn't you two say anything when Mom was ordering? You have to pay attention."

"I didn't think she'd go off the rails," her father said.

"The menu said no changes," his wife said. "You like anchovies, and the only way to get them was on the arugula pizza. The other pizza is andouille sausage and potato. It was the closest I could get to pepperoni, but it did say it was organic and cruelty-free. Who knew sausage could be cruel in the first place?" She laughed and looked around the silent table.

"Fascists," said Paulie as he took a slice of the andouille pie, eating most of it in two large bites.

"There's no getting around cruelty if the pig had to die for our sausage," said Evelyn.

"Can I get you anything else?" Glory asked. Evelyn blushed and shook her head no.

"Another drink," her father said. "Straight bourbon this time."

"We have a nice whiskey distilled locally," said Glory. "Can I get you a taste?"

"No, you can get me a glass of Jim Beam over rocks."

Evelyn tried to catch Glory's eye to smile, as in, what can you do? But Glory had turned on her boot heels to the bar. "I'll see what we've got."

"Did you know that formaldehyde is an appetite stimulant?" Evelyn asked.

"Bring it on," said Paulie with a full mouth.

"Here," their mom said, trying to push a slice onto Evelyn's plate.

"I can't have any pizza, mom. I'm gluten free, remember? No wheat?"

"Oh, I forgot," she said. "Why didn't you remind me when

I ordered it?"

"Why didn't you ask where I wanted to go on my birthday? Because it certainly wouldn't have been an artisanal pizza and oyster bistro. I can't do gluten and I'm allergic to shellfish. That's why I had the salad."

"But you hardly touched it."

"She likes being a victim," said Paulie, reaching for another piece.

"Martyr," said her mother. "Not victim."

"More for us," said her father, as he picked arugula off his pizza slice.

Evelyn leaned back in her chair with her arms crossed. She glanced down at her watch, then pushed her shirt sleeve up and envisioned a tattoo. She liked Glory's tendrils and crows, but she was not so sure about the skulls. Maybe if you lived above death you had to make friends with it.

"Don't just sit there acting pious," her father said to her. "Look what you're doing to your mother." Evelyn turned to her mother, who lifted up her head in mid-bite at the sound of her name.

"Look what *you're* doing to her," said Evelyn, then under her breath she muttered the word "thug."

"What was that?" her father asked. His face was a roasted, hot color and Evelyn thought he might be sitting too close to the pizza oven. He undid the top button of his shirt.

"You're a thug," she repeated. "A bully and a thug."

His nostril veins became pronounced and when he opened his mouth, his face swung loose from his cheekbones. Evelyn braced herself as he began to stand, but still no sound came out. In her mind there were only bubbles, bubbles escaping from his nose and ears, floating up and bursting before they reached the ceiling.

"Henry, Henry, what's wrong?" her mother asked.

"What the fuck?" asked Paulie. "Dad, what are you doing?"

Evelyn stood and she and her father stared at one another as he slowly sank, drifting to the floor instead of rising to the surface. He swallowed air in sharp spasms and clung onto the edge of the table like a Gila monster, and when he lost his grip he clutched at the white tablecloth, pulling the hot pizzas towards him. Evelyn grasped her side of the linen with both hands to keep everything from falling on him and was still holding on when the staff came running over. Glory stood next to Evelyn and helped her, as if the tablecloth were a lifeline to her father, paying out cloth as he finally settled on the floorboards. Then Glory snatched the pizza pedestals before they fell off the edge as another server shoved the table aside. They all backed up for the manager, who was rushing towards them with a defibrillator under her arm, as if heading into war.

Evelyn's mother turned to Glory and screamed, "Is he going to die? Is he dying?"

The manager read the directions on the side of the defibrillator box while the bartender checked her father's airway, then tore open his jacket and shirt, exposing his flesh.

"I know dead people," said Glory. "He's not. Good color."

The manager placed the insulating pads on her father's naked chest and administered the first electric shock, and Evelyn imagined a flash of light cutting through the darkness within. But nothing happened. Nothing changed. Evelyn could hear sirens in the distance, and then she started shaking.

Huldufólk

ASTRID, THEIR ICELANDIC tour guide, was so white her head seemed disembodied from her black Gore-Texed torso. Nary a suggestion of yellow in her hair, no pink to her skin, but it could have been the lighting, or more accurately, its lack. The entire busload of tourists knew one another only by flashlight. It had been dark when they boarded in Reykjavik, it was darker still an hour away from the artificial glow of the city, the better to view the aurora borealis streaking white and green in the sky. Released from the bus, they had arranged themselves on rocks in the field, silhouettes bundled against the cold, and when the first Day-Glo glimmer appeared on the celestial canvas, they gasped with awe. Except for Cuddy, for whom there was something disturbing about the ghostly colors and erratic waves. Intellectually she understood it was an atmospheric phenomena of electrical discharge, but the lights seemed to pulse like a medical device monitoring a body in the throes of crisis, and all she could think of was death.

Another device exhibiting distress was her new camera. She had read the manual on how to take pictures of the night sky but it failed her. Or she failed it. Either way, the screen was coming up blank. As others adjusted their tripods and held iPhones to the sky, she sat alone on her unforgiving rock, her down jacket pulled tight around her, and thought. Here she was travelling alone on a three-day Groupon tour to Iceland in hopes that the trip might pull her out of her post-divorce funk, but so much for the power of natural wonders. She had a cold butt and a numb nose and no epiphany to speak of. As with her spouse, she had chosen her trip poorly, and as with her marriage, she knew it from the start. On the red-eye over she'd watched her flight progress across the entertainment screen in growing apprehension with every shipwreck marked along the route. The Titanic, the Lusitania, others she'd never even heard of before but now, at 36,000 feet over the icy Atlantic, she was being forced to consider. Granted, there were no landmarks because there was no land, but really. Shipwrecks? Did Icelandair think the passengers were so totally without imagination that they couldn't transpose ship to plane? But once she hit ground, it suddenly seemed in character. This was clearly a pragmatic people who faced their problems with no sugar-coating, not even in their public art. Bronze statues of slump-shouldered humans trod through Reykjavik's city square, walking aimlessly through life, cut off at the knees. When she got to the hotel, the first thing she saw when she turned on the TV was a public service ad that showed a woman too depressed to go shopping for furniture. This woman, too, was slumped, but she had a husband who knew what to do and got her to the clinic in time. No waiting. Even at the famous Blue Lagoon spa that day, people trudged through the steamy water like zombies, in slow motion, their faces muddied white with silica masks.

But Cuddy had no husband, no one to pull her up off of the sofa and back into life. Quite the opposite. It had been her husband who had pushed her down into the sofa and nearly smothered her with the cushions. Metaphorically speaking. She put her mittened hands to her face and exhaled warmth into the wool. In the darkness around her she heard oohs and aahs grow in intensity with every new splash of colored light as if it were a choreographed fireworks show. But the universe was not so tidy as all that. There was no plan. She tucked her hands under her armpits. "Enough already," she said, but her words fell on the stony ground. At one a.m. she was the first one back on the bus, fighting a fatigue that had nothing to do with the hour. *Weltschmerz.* That was the word for it. She was definitely suffering from weltschmerz, roughly translated as having a weary heart, trapped in the space between the real world and the one in her head, one of those insanely specific conditions of the soul that the Germans loved to name and catalogue. She should have gone to Berlin instead. She could have seen the Wall.

As they all settled in their bus seats, Astrid made multiple trips up and down the aisle with her clipboard, and when the doors closed she welcomed them back. Her face was so softly illuminated by a pinlight on her clipboard she seemed to be addressing them from inside a crystal ball.

"I know to you we must seem fussy doing these head counts over and over," she said, "but I will tell you why. Two years ago there was a night when for some reason the bus driver was also the guide, and he was unsure of his count. When it was time to go back to Reykjavik it looked to him like everyone was in the bus and he started to leave, but someone said, wait, there was a woman in a black jacket who hadn't gotten on the bus yet, so they waited. Then the driver got the searchlight and started looking in the fields and the bathrooms. He could not find her and everyone on the bus got very nervous, and one by one, they got out to look for this woman. The driver calls the police and they start searching too. Two hours later, a woman in the tour who had been searching went back in the bus to get her black jacket, which she had been wearing earlier, and put it on, and that is when someone 'found' her. She hadn't recognized the description of herself. It was four a.m. by the time they were on the road back to Reykjavik. So that is why I must keep counting your heads."

"That's me," Cuddy thought as the bus finally headed into the darkness. "I'm that woman out looking for herself. The woman who can't see herself for who she is."

Earlier, in the half-light of the Icelandic winter day, Cuddy had walked in the depression between two tectonic plates at the Thingvellir National Park. It seems she had walked in that place her entire life, and now the universe had to step in with its lights and colors and natural phenomena to grab her by the shoulders and shake her awake. Pay attention! Pay attention or pay the price. Then they'd motored to a geyser field, where under a low sky, they watched a series of hydrothermal explosions, from bubbling mud-pots to big cauldrons that spewed energy into the air with weightless abandon. Yet they did not exhaust themselves, for after a short rest they would go at it again. She saw the original geyser, from which all others took their name. It was Iceland's only exported word, and meant "to gush." In a frozen world, steam rose in tides from an earth born of volcanoes, an entire country boiling right beneath the surface with potential and energy. The world spoke volumes, but she had watched the geysers, the lights, and the space where continents collide without thinking they had anything to do with her.

"I must change my life," she said to herself.

On the dark drive back to the hotel through the frosted lava desert, Cuddy rested her head against the cold window and felt herself glow with fire from deep inside. She had so much to do when she returned to the States. So many doors to open. Classes, dating services, books, plays, volunteer work. She was not a defeated leftover from a sour marriage, she was only gathering her strength to begin again. First off, she would stop sitting in front of the TV every night scrolling through reality shows and dramas of calculated lives, endings with no loose ends, fueling her discontent. Such a waste. She would get out and make a difference and help others, not just to find her place in the world, if there was such a thing, but to discover the world in her heart. No more whining, no slumping about.

When the bus arrived at the hotel, people gathered their coats and bags and dragged themselves up to their rooms for some sleep, but not Cuddy. She was exhilarated and could not close her eyes. She felt alive, no longer blinded by familiar surroundings and established habit, and wished she could stay in Iceland forever. She regretted, now, that she had not joined a couple of the other women on the tour for a quick excursion to visit the Phallological Museum downtown, where taxidermied penises, from house mouse to humpback, filled the rooms, including mythic penises from a merman and a troll. It sounded silly, but they'd had fun. Another growth experience missed, but she wouldn't let something like that slip through her hands again. At the airport the next morning, she stopped at the duty-free shop and bought a sky-blue Icelandic wool sweater for her niece, and a bottle of brennivín, the indigenous alcohol, for herself. She would have a party. A big party. On the flight home, she did not spend the hours staring at a screen, but at the clouds.

When she got back to the office, a dead-end administrative job that would have to be reconsidered along with the rest, she told Irma the story about the woman who was looking for herself. As she prattled on about Iceland and its profound effect upon her, Irma took out her phone and tapped around a bit. "I've heard that before," she said and showed Cuddy. "That missing tourist of yours pops up on the internet every couple of years. No name, no date, just 'somewhere' in Iceland. I think it's, what's that word? Epical?"

"Apocryphal," said Cuddy, staring at the screen.

"It probably never happened," said Irma and she clicked off her phone. "But it's a good story."

Cuddy continued to stare at the empty space where the phone used to be.

"Drink after work?" said Irma. "I can catch you up."

Cuddy shook her head. "I've got plans."

When she got home to her apartment that night she switched on the light and stood there, disoriented. How had it come to be that she had wandered into this life? No chair was inviting and even her books on the shelf looked on loan. There were no photographs on the walls, no sign of humanity in the art. Even the Icelanders with their bronze depressives wandering the city square at least acknowledged the common struggle. She went to the bedroom where her carry-on duffel lay open on the bed, still unpacked, as untouched as the boxes from her divorce two years before. She unzipped the bag and there on the top was the child's sweater, the long fibers of the blue wool like a pelt. She pressed it against her face and breathed in the scent of the Icelandic sheep, living against all odds in a harsh climate, surviving on moss, then folded it back up in its tissue. She would give the sweater to her niece now and not wait for a holiday. Underneath, wrapped in layers of bags, was the bottle of brennivín. In Iceland she had started the day with the traditional iced shot of cod liver oil and ended it with a frigid shot of brennivín. Like the country itself it was strong brew, but it had grown on her. She unscrewed the top to sniff the potent distillation of caraway seed and the trip gushed out, filling the room.

Something else had happened on that bus ride back to Reykjavik, and in her giddiness over the lost woman she had almost forgot. They were driving along and she was jostled back to her surroundings by an abrupt swerve in the road around a boulder, and then the road continued straight again. It was odd enough that Astrid felt it was due some explanation. It was some explanation. "In the construction of the road," she said, "the builders move the boulder out of the way, and calamities begin to fall. A flying iron cog here, a missing finger there, scalding hot tar, a broken leg, then another. This goes on for days. When the crew's children came down with mysterious illnesses, the government realized elves were living in the rock and did not want their home disturbed. The rock was moved back to where it was, the road was built around it, and the children got well."

The tour group hardly knew how to respond, whether in amusement or sympathy. Astrid seemed to be all seriousness in the telling, as in, the elves, but of course. Huldufólk the Icelanders called them. The hidden people. It was a tough and brutal world, Iceland. The black earth boiled with uncertainty and the skies were filled with menacing lights. Who, living in such a harsh land, could not believe in a force greater than themselves?

If these pragmatic people could believe in elves, Cuddy could believe in an apocryphal woman. She could believe in herself. She put the bottle in the freezer, because it can never be served too cold and she planned to invite friends over very soon. She would surround herself with life. As she prepared her dinner, she reached for the TV remote by habit, and put it back down. "No," she said. "No more." She would be the boulder that forced the road to change its path, alive inside and full of elves.

Sunk

ON MONDAY, BRAD came home from work humming to himself, but at the path to his door the hum drained to cracked hardpan. The sky was washed in purple, so that the picture window was as reflective as a mirror. His house had changed but he could not say how. "Must be the light," he decided, then went inside to his wife, Edna, and his small child, Oliver, and forgot all about it. But on Tuesday night it was as changed, if not more so. "Something is definitely off," he said to Edna, who was in the kitchen scraping dried mac and cheese into the disposal. "I'll say something's off," she said, without looking up. On Wednesday, he averted his eyes as he approached the house, but on Thursday morning he obsessed on it. "It's tilting," he said out loud, and stuck a yardstick up against the concrete foundation. It looked perpendicular, but what did he know? He was a bean counter, not an architect. That night it was too dark to tell what was what, but on Friday morning he detected a sliver of light between the house and the ruler. "Could be the

stick," he told himself, then ran for the bus. On Saturday, he offered
to rake leaves so he could watch for any sudden movement. "Be my
guest," said Edna, pushing Oliver outside to jump in the leaf pile,
which never materialized. Brad was too busy studying the space
between stick and house. At lunchtime, Edna called them in, but
there was no "them." It took many tense minutes to find Oliver
who had wandered down the block, making Edna irritable. She
refused to join Brad in the inspection of a hairline fracture on the
kitchen ceiling. "You want to invest coincidence with meaning," she
said, and he wasn't quite sure what she meant, if anything. That
night in bed he heard the house creak like the dry snapping of
bones. "The heating system," he told himself, but when he checked
the thermostat Sunday morning, it wasn't even on.

On the second Monday, Brad examined the yardstick on leaving for work and on his return. The space of light had grown from
a sliver to a slender wedge. He was sure. He stood under the ashy
sky until Oliver came to the window and pressed his open mouth
against the glass like a Moray eel. At work on Tuesday morning,
he joked with Marvin in technology. "My house is sinking." Ha,
ha. "Sounds like normal settling to me," said Marvin. "Ah," said
Brad, and celebrated with a jelly donut. Then Marvin told him
about a friend whose aunt's house fell in a sinkhole. "The earth just
swallowed it up," he said, and red jelly oozed from Brad's clenched
fist. On Wednesday night, Brad told Edna he was going to hire

a structural engineer. "To make sure it's just normal settling." He did not look up from his beef stew when he said those words, but he felt Edna's eyes upon him. "Nor-mal," Oliver whispered to the turnip on his fork. On Thursday, Brad asked Marvin if he knew any structural engineers. "A great guy," Marv said, and gave him the number. That night Brad told Edna that the man would be there Friday, and she blinked. The next morning, before she got out of bed, she turned to Brad and said, "Have you thought that it might be you, and not the house?" He had no answer to that, so she got up and made French toast.

There was a note on the kitchen table when Brad got home Friday night. "Everything that needs to be said has already been said. But since you weren't listening, everything must be said again." Brad skipped to the end. Edna had run off with the structural engineer taking Oliver with her. There was an addendum in a different hand at the bottom: The engineer would send a full report in a few weeks, with the bill.

It was Monday night again but Brad did not come home from work because he had not gone to work. His sense of time passing had become an unwavering echo of heartbeats. A webbed aluminum chair on the lawn was his citadel, where he took the measure of the world. Wrapped in a scratchy blanket, he watched the stars swirl above in wonder. "There are nine galaxies for each one of us," he said, and felt the cheek-flapping speed of the planet rushing through space. He clutched the cold metal chair and began to hum like a rocket, tilting rapidly into the unknown, free of gravity altogether, already missing the earth disappearing below.

Piece of
History

Piece of History – Restored Mill tucked into a narrow gorge, sitting alone with an undisturbed view of the waterfalls. The constant roar soothes body and mind. The combination of glass, timber, and stone creates an unforgettable set of living spaces. Call Leslie at Brancaleone Realty today! Don't miss out!

Warren stood looking through the picture window at the intensity of the natural world, the gray water exploding down the falls, thick and churning with dirt, eating away at both sides of the gorge. What strength. What power! If the old wooden water wheel were still attached, what a sight that would be.

A clod of mud still clung to the sleeve of his camouflage rain gear and he flicked it into the flagstone hearth, a direct hit on the damp white logs. From above, rubber-booted feet pounded down the stairs and then he heard his wife run into the kitchen. "Mica," he called, but she seemed to not hear him. He couldn't even hear himself, what with the rushing torrent below and the rain slamming on the slate roof above. Not to mention Fergus yapping at his side. He raised his voice when he saw Mica dart through the hall again.

"Wait a minute, Mica! Stop right there."

She didn't stop so much as redirect her energy, whipping into the living room as if she might charge right over him, clutching baby Fay under one arm like a pink football. In the other hand she held an unzipped diaper bag. Mica was tall and usually quite beautiful, but right now, dressed in a yellow rain suit with her blond hair loose and unbrushed, she looked like a bedraggled Valkyrie. She stopped abruptly in the middle of the timber-framed room and looked up at the wrought-iron chandelier, taking a deliberate step out from under it before turning her frantic attention on him.

"This had better be about death or dog shit, Warren, otherwise I don't want to hear about it."

Warren was so thrown off by her coarse attack that he forgot what it was he wanted to say. Then, with a jolt, she dropped the diaper bag to the floor and headed to the leather sofa, upon which sat the baby's car seat. "Sweet Jesus," she said, as if she'd just spotted a lifeboat, and moved swiftly to strap Fay into her little carrier. Soft plastic squares of disposable diapers had been thrown from the bag on impact and were now spread out around her feet. Without even looking, she kicked one out of her way with her rainboot and it skidded across the wide pine floor. She stepped on a rubber giraffe toy and it squeaked in terror, but she didn't even seem to notice, so intent was her struggle with the car-seat straps. "And shut Fergus up. Aren't things bad enough?"

"Things aren't bad," Warren said, flustered by her irrational behavior. "You're just making them seem that way."

She glanced up at him with such scorn he wondered who she was. He was too old for such hysterics. In a weak moment of loneliness a few years ago, he'd been fooled by her looks, mistaking a high forehead for intelligence. When in truth, her blond eyebrows were so transparent they only gave her that impression. It's not that she was stupid, it was just that she refused to see the world as a place of wonder and learning. He read books, went to foreign films and museums; her only concerns were making sure she wrung the most comfort and pleasure from the towel of life as she could. He put his hand down to placate Fergus, his black lab, who, like his wife, was overreacting to the sight of rising water. The dog increased his barking at his master's touch. "Get a grip, Fergus," Warren said, roughly. "You're a water dog. Act like one."

"Well I'm no water dog," said Mica, flooding the room with waves of irritation. "I'm out of here." She knelt down and began to crawl rapidly around on the floor, sweeping the diapers back into the quilted bag. She tossed the giraffe to Fergus and it landed with a human noise, which stunned the dog into silence. Warren walked over to help Mica with the mess she'd created, but when he peeked at Fay through the muffled wrappings of her outfit, she looked at him with such a furious little face that he refused to bend.

"Mica, I want you to stay," he said. "It's safer here than out there."

He'd just been outside to collect water for flushing the toilets. It was no weather for traveling. A few minutes of exposure and even his waterproof garments were soaked through. The rain flowed from the sky with such force that his buckets were half full by the time he found a working downspout. The earth had kept slipping out from under his wellies as he squished about for stable ground, trying to find secure footing. On his way back to the door, a fierce wind whipped debris all around him until he felt like he was in a blender. He touched the top of his head where a small sharp branch had found a target.

Mica stood, ignoring Warren. She picked up the baby carrier in one hand and adjusted the diaper bag on her shoulder with the other as she ran to the hallway. "Jason!" she called up the stairs.

She collapsed against a timbered post for support, almost panting, and Warren worried about her mental state. As her husband, he should protect her from herself. Jason ran down the stairs with a struggling three-year old Brenda in his arms, whose pale face was fringed in reddish curls. Jason was seventeen, Warren's lanky and laconic son from his first marriage, home from Andover for his monthly visit with Dad. He was a good kid, and Warren had hoped they could do some father-son activities on the property that weekend—make a stone wall, clear some brush. Instead, they had spent every minute since they got there the night before just trying to maintain. How could he have known that a week of hard rain in the mountains would mean no electricity, and ironically, because the pump depended on it, no water either? Under normal circumstances, they wouldn't need heat, but the wet weather made for a cold June. Worse, the metal chimney cap must have blown off during the storm, allowing water to cascade down the inner walls of the flue. So in effect, they were camping out without a fire, eating cold hash from a can and washing up with baby wipes.

"Brenda, pumpkin, are you ready to go bye-bye?" Mica asked in a nervous singsong voice. Brenda's soft patter was drowned out by a sudden surge of rain.

"Jason, stay here with your old man," said Warren. "We can play some cards. Mica, is there an intact deck lying around here somewhere?"

"Um, Dad…" said Jason, who stood taller than his father at half the weight. Brenda yanked at his long hair, still struggling to be free, then jammed her froggie boots into his ribs. "Ouch," he said, and strengthened his grip on her.

Mica gave Warren a withering look, then turned to her stepson. "Jason," she said. "Take Fay to the car. Brenda, come to mommy. Stop fussing, we're going to be fine." Mica held the bucket of baby out to Jason and he happily passed Brenda from his hip to Mica's.

"Fergie, Fergie, Fergie," Brenda wailed, her short legs now firmly attached around Mica's waist, her arms reaching out and waving wildly at the dog, who was finally pacified, chewing on the giraffe. Why doesn't she call Daddy, Daddy, Daddy, Warren wondered. She was the reason he and Mica had gotten married in the first place. He'd been trapped by biology. Mica said she wanted the child, when he knew that what she'd really wanted was him, the father of the child. He'd given up his freedom for them, so he'd better make it worth the sacrifice. He was about to stretch his arms out to Brenda for a hug when he felt a ripping sensation run through the building. He looked out the window to see a clapboard get tossed in the air by the water like a plaything, then disappear downstream. They all stared in wonder.

"Holy shit," said Jason, clutching the car seat to his chest. "Was that us?"

"Shit!" Brenda screamed. "Shit!" Mica pressed her cheek on Brenda's head without correcting the potty language.

"A loose board," Warren said. "After the rain stops, we'll just tack up a new..." and he dismissed the rest of his sentence with a flick of his hand, as if it were too obvious to go on.

"This place is sketchy, Dad," Jason said. "Let's go and leave it to the ghost."

"Ghost!" yelled Brenda. "Ghost!"

"It's okay, pumpkin," Mica said to her, with no conviction whatsoever.

"Jason," said Warren. "Brenda's upset enough without *that*."

"That" was the real estate agent's ghoulish belief that you couldn't sell an old mill without a ghost attached. The truth was—as always—a simple matter of physics. Yes, occasionally they'd get a chill up their spines, but the cause was far from supernatural. Structures built over water, whether they be caves or castles or mills, sent out electric vibes, a particular energy that made them feel "haunted." Monks had always sought such places out to enhance the religious experience. In fact, white water produced negative ions which cleared the air and make people feel well, the very opposite of haunted. He felt great when he was here.

"Hurry," Mica said to Jason. "Get Fay in the car and start it up. I have to grab my phone. If we drive far enough away from this black crevice we might actually get some reception."

Warren knelt on one knee to pat Fergus as a reward for staying calm. "Shush, shush, ssh..." he said as he ran his hand over the smooth damp fur. Fergus was a fine dog, named after King Fergus I of Scotland, a contemporary of Alexander the Great. A warrior for the ages. Warren rubbed his jaw and his hand smelled of wet dog. He should get into dry clothes himself, but he'd wait until his family was gone. While Mica was tossing things around in the kitchen, he stood up and tried to sneak a look outside to see where the clapboard had been torn off, and he was startled to see the water surging right below the window. Maybe Mica was right to get out now. For all he knew, there were no clapboards at all left below the high water mark. At the showing, he'd noted signs of erosion on the walls of the gorge but he'd thought they were ancient. He'd noted, too, that the stone foundation was built right into the side of the gorge, but the stream had seemed thin and inconsequential, and the boulders between it and the mill huge. The agent had said there was occasional flooding, but that it was very exciting, "worth paying double for," she'd joked.

The situation was no better behind the house. Runoff swept down from the road above, and what had started as inconsequential rivulets joined together to become a single destructive force, gouging out gullies on either side of the building. But certainly this had happened before. He'd just never thought to ask. The gristmill had been built in 1878, and if it had lasted this long without being washed away, it wasn't going to now—Al Gore's nonsense about global warming to the contrary. These were natural cyclical changes that came and went over time, and Gore failed to grasp the big picture. The water was violent, yes, rising, certainly, and fast. But it would also recede on its own, as it always had, and surely would. Soon. He would stay and watch the transition. He rubbed his bristly jaw. Like Nixon, his old nemesis from his liberal youth, he had to shave twice a day, but the thought of splashing cold water on his face was not very appetizing. Not that he'd mind looking like a mountain man, but his facial hair was coming in gray these days and it made him feel old.

He was still rubbing his face and thinking when Mica came back with Brenda on her hip. She shoved the cellphone into a zippered pocket and stopped at the front door with her hand on the knob. "Aren't you going to do anything to help?" she shouted over the sound of raging water. "Or are you just going to stand there like a statue?"

Warren contemplated, and did not move. She'd need him. They would all need him. But it was impossible for him to go along. It was one thing for women and children to run to higher ground, but he was committed to seeing this thing through. "I'd better stay here, hold down the fort." He chuckled, as if he'd said something amusing. "Got to protect our piece of history."

For a moment, Mica looked like she just might spit. "*Piece of history*," she hissed, as if she were saying *kiss my ass*. "We're going while we still can, Warren. Come, don't come, I don't care. I've got the children to think of. But remember, you won't have a car when I go, and I'm not coming back to get you."

Before he could respond, the storm door opened out with such force it almost pulled her with it. Jason had lost control of it trying to get back in, and the two of them had to pull together to close it again. Brenda screamed "*No, no, no,*" as if she could stop the wind with words. Jason was soaked and streaked with mud.

"Mica, I, um, turned the car around so we could just shoot out. It's going to be hard getting the car up there unless we build up steam."

Warren was pleased to hear Jason be so practical. The experience would be good for him, make him more of a man. It was time the boy learned that it was perfectly natural for events to swing from crisis to resolution, and back again. There was no need for panic. The wheel was just slightly turned a bit in favor of chaos right now, but he wouldn't call it dire. Not by a long shot. It was ready to swing right on back again.

"Dad, uh, you'd better come with us. It's getting wild around here. Like really deep grooves. I think I can see under the foundation."

"Since when are you an engineer?" Warren snapped. "The last I heard, you couldn't even crack a B in calculus."

Jason gave his father a cross between a sneer and a shrug, then turned to take Brenda from Mica's hip. He left without saying goodbye. "You go and help your stepmother with the kids," Warren called after him, as if this were all his idea to begin with, as if they were all just following his orders. But Jason was long gone.

Mica adjusted the hood on her head. "Are you happy?" she asked, her mouth a tight line across her face.

He turned away to look out the window. It was harsh, maybe, what he'd said to Jason, but it was not for a son to tell a father what to do.

"Fergus," she said, and patted her rain pants. "Let's go."

Fergus leaped up, but Warren grabbed hold of his collar. "He's *my* dog, and he's staying with me."

Mica looked as if she might stand her ground and fight, but then a casement window upstairs came loose and started banging open and closed like artillery fire. The sound jolted her out the door, which slammed so hard behind her that Warren could feel it in his spine.

Fergus struggled and whined. "They'll be back, buddy," Warren said, but the dog was unconvinced, twisting around to free himself of his collar. "Go ahead," said Warren, releasing him. "You're all a bunch of babies." Fergus ran to the hall, whined at the door, then stretched out in front of it, resting his head on his front paws. Water seeped in from under the door. The dog watched the rivulets disappear under the welcome mat and twitched his ears to the sounds of the Lexus making an attempt up the hill, the grinding of gears, the slipping of mud, rocks skidding down to the parking area. Warren was well aware that there was hardly any dirt left on the driveway for the tires to dig into. It was all water and stone now. The whirring of the wheels sounded increasingly desperate. Mica was a tough little nut, he had to give her that. He wondered if he should go out there and help. Was it his duty, even though he didn't approve? Reluctantly, he knew that to go outside and help them escape would only put his stamp of approval on the whole business. He relaxed his shoulders and took off his rain jacket. It had been such an effort to talk over the noise that it seemed almost quiet when he no longer had to struggle to be heard.

He looked around. He'd never been here by himself before and it was a pleasant change, even if the circumstances were tense at that particular moment. He liked the way the room was open to the peaked roofline, leaving thick structural beams extending from one sleeping loft to the other. He appreciated that in the first restoration in the 70s, some old hippie had the foresight to remove the huge paddled wheel from its exposed position outside and mount it on the rear interior wall. It was so graphic, so at home. The mill already felt like home to him too, more so than their duplex in the city. He ran his hand over the slab of blond wood that served as the mantel for the stone fireplace and thought of trying another fire, but water continued to pour down the chimney in sheets. What a rain. A hundred-year rain and he was a part of it. History, it was nothing to scoff at.

There was a low rumble, and he wondered if it was thunder, or was the car actually working its way up the hill? He took off his water repellent pants, and he got a chill as the air hit his damp khakis. He felt a slight tremor under his feet, as if the building had shifted in some fundamental way, but he put that thought out of his mind. This was not a house built on sand, it was built on rock. Good old native fieldstone. Posts and sills of massive pines. The infrastructure was unimpeachable. In fact, the storm might have a cleansing effect, showing him where the weak spots were so he could replace them. When this was over, the old mill would be better than ever, ready to withstand another century, a monument to American industry. He ran both hands over his khakis and looked longingly at the hearth. But the wood was soaked and he didn't want to go out to the shed while his family was still out there. He'd wait them out.

Fergus stood up and his wet ears were cocked. Curious as Warren was, there was no way to check on their progress. The windows looked out over the gorge, not behind at the wall of hill, where the dirt drive zigzagged up the incline. Then they heard the spinning of wheels pick up again. Mica must be beside herself with fury by now. She never wanted to be here in the first place. She wanted a second home in some sort of vacation development, with a pool and a rec center for the kids. She wanted people close by, as if he weren't enough. But he'd stuck to his guns. He wasn't going to go against his convictions and be pressured into some quasi-retirement playtime village. He needed a challenge, something to reflect his renegade personality. He wanted to leave his mark. "We're going up to the mill this weekend," he'd announced to the office, and the staff had looked at him with awe. When he told Mica that, she snorted and said they were paid to look at him with awe. She was a very pessimistic person when it came right down to it.

He heard a crash and saw a tumble of rocks shoot off the edge of the gorge and down to the water not so very far below. The place was lousy with rocks, in fact, the whole county was covered with stone farms. There was no money to be made off the land around here, except for lumbering. He'd felled a few trees of his own lately.

Not by his own hand, of course, but by his orders. It was a good plan at heart, but now, watching the topsoil slide by in a slurry, he realized he should have opened up the view more slowly. The arborist had warned him about not culling the old trees so aggressively, and he certainly shouldn't have cleared away all the underbrush. But what reasonable man would have believed that a few roots were all that was holding the hill together?

Fergus began barking again and the door blew open, straining at the hinges. Warren got to his feet in a panic, then exhaled in relief. Mica came running back in, soaked and panting. She had the baby carrier; behind her, Jason had Brenda. It was his little family back again. He had won. They were going to weather this together. The door slammed shut behind them without their help and Jason sat Brenda down on the slate floor of the entryway, then he went back outside in a blast of wind before Warren could say something cheery. He didn't want Jason to stay mad at him. Brenda's yellow-ducky raincoat had unsnapped, and he thought he could see her wet neck pulsating with fear. Poor baby. He went to pick her up but Mica stepped between them. She was trying to catch her breath.

"Give up?" he asked.

"The car," she said, in between breaths. "It slipped sideways and a wheel got stuck in the culvert. I almost ran over Jason trying to push."

"I hope you're satisfied," he said. "I'll take care of the car later, when the rain stops."

"You do that, Warren," she said.

Fay began to cry, but when Warren went to get her, Mica pointedly moved the car-seat to the far corner of the hall while she rummaged through the closet. He stood at the doorway, stunned to see her pull out a backpack and a front pack.

"What do you think you're doing?" he demanded.

"We're walking to safety." She yanked off her slicker and attached the front pack to her body.

"No, you're not."

She stared at him while she snapped a buckle at her waist. "You are worse than useless, Warren, you are a dangerous impediment. Jason is getting rope and we're pulling ourselves up the hill through the trees."

There was a loud crunch and the building shook. Mica screamed, setting off Brenda, Fay, and Fergus. Warren reached out to comfort her, then thought better of it. There was no need to panic. The mill had been shaking all day from the wind, this was just more of the same. He put his hands in his damp pockets, as if feeling one's home move about were an everyday occurrence. "Don't worry," he said, feeling a chill on his arms. "This place is built like a bomb shelter. It's not going anywhere." He paused for effect. "And neither are you."

"It's going to the bottom of the gorge, you idiot," Mica shouted as she squatted to undo the baby's straps. "If you're going to chain yourself to this sinking ship, you're going down alone."

"Where did Jason go?" Warren asked. "He's my responsibility and he's staying here with me."

"Oh shut up," said Mica, gesturing wildly. She stood up and ran into the bathroom and came back with a towel to dry the baby's face, then Brenda's, who continued to sit in the puddle Jason had placed her in. She was very quiet.

"I'll help you get them into dry clothes," said Warren. "Then we can play some games until the electricity comes back on. Take our minds off the storm. Maybe it's time to teach Brenda chess."

"Don't you touch my children," she said, pulling Brenda to her, and laying a hand on the baby's stomach. "*Leave us alone.*"

Warren blinked. How had they gotten to this point? He'd started the day with such boyish excitement. Yes, it was bad when they arrived the night before in the storm to find no electricity, but in the morning, even before he opened his eyes he recognized that the day had a completely different tenor. Life had been stripped down to the bare facts. He'd risen up off the futon and punched the air. It was just the feeling he'd been after when he bought the mill, like owning your own fire engine or ambulance.

"Mommy?" asked Brenda, oddly calm.

Mica was short with her as she struggled with the zipper on Fay's suit. "Yes?"

Brenda patted the puddle with both hands. "Rain is like water, isn't it?"

Mica paused and looked at her daughter. "Usually, honey," she said, standing up with Fay in her arms. "But in this case, no. This rain is not like anything else."

Warren, who'd been smiling at his daughter, frowned at Mica. "Christ, only you could take the cute words of an innocent kid and twist them around to suit your own purposes."

"Open your eyes, Warren. What's needed here is a dose of reality."

In a burst of wind and a silver blast of water, Jason appeared at the door with a coil of rope. He did not even look at his father, but quickly went to work tying it around his own waist, then passed the end to Mica to tie around herself. Warren was disgusted with them both, and went back to the window where he could experience the storm in peace. Out of the corner of his eye, he saw Jason take the baby and slip her into Mica's front pack, as Mica zipped the slicker over her and Fay both. Mica squeezed Brenda into her aluminum-frame pack and helped Jason lift it onto his back. When she put the plastic poncho over them, the hood covered Brenda's head, but not Jason's. She grabbed a Red Sox baseball cap from a hook and put it on him.

They all jumped when they heard a tremendous cracking, but it was not the mill. Warren, standing closest to the window, had seen the whole thing, but had been unable to open his mouth. Or, more correctly, he opened his mouth and nothing came out. A giant pine in the side yard had tipped over, its water-logged roots having separated from the earth, then dropped with a single tumble into the gorge. It missed their roof by a foot. The tree was now firmly lodged between a submerged rock and the mill foundation, at an angle that caused it to reach out across the gorge, creating a sweeper to catch the flotilla of debris. It was slightly downstream of the mill. If enough flotsam built up it would create a dam, forming a lake, just where he stood.

The door slammed. They were gone. He went after them and opened the door, and as he did, Fergus snuck out between his legs and ran ahead to the family, frantically slipping on the mud. They had already begun their ascent, crawling up the steep incline, hand over hand, pulling themselves on a rope that Jason had tied off to trees all the way up to the road. It was like an Antarctic camp, with lifelines leading to all points so no one would be lost by whiteouts. "Mica," he called out, but the words got battered to the ground by the rain. His family became blurry silhouettes against the hill, tied together and pulling together, deserting him. The dog had no hands to pull himself up by the rope, so Jason and Mica took turns shoving him along, to keep him from backsliding.

Against his better judgment, Warren was impressed that they were making headway. It was unlikely they'd get anywhere, but good for them for trying! He waved but they never looked back. The wind was blowing water on him, soaking the front of his sweatshirt. He got the storm door closed but when he tried to shut the inner door, he found that the sill had become swollen. His breath was labored by the time he got it latched. It was all just an exercise in futility. They'd be right back. With no car, small children, and an old dog, where could they go? The nearest neighbor was a mile through the woods. Town was miles away. There was no shoulder on the road. He reached down to pet Fergus, then remembered he was gone.

When he reentered the living room, the light in the room had turned the color of strong tea even though sunset was hours away. What meteorological event was preceded by funny light? Tornado? Hurricane? Fine. Bring it on. He thought of the men who used to work the mill, flirting daily with treacherous fly wheels and gnashing gears. Their livelihood depended on the power of the water, water which at that moment was pressing hard against the building, a fallible thing made by man, yes, but a structure that would withstand the test. In his bones, he felt the force of the rain hitting the roof above. He looked outside at the stream, swollen to the size of a river, and just as he did, fistfuls of green spew whipped off the choppy water and splattered onto the glass.

The banging of the window upstairs continued, and Warren knew he'd have to do something about it. Not yet, though. He'd deal with it soon, but he was tired now. He went to sit down in one of the heavy leather chairs by the window to think, and felt himself thrown back into it. He held his breath. He could not tell if that had been the building adjusting itself, or him off-balance. He felt dizzy. For a brief moment he had a vision, more like a "sensation," of the room filled with sturdy working men, feeding grist to the mill. Sweating like animals, cursing like stevedores, servicing the grindstones, trying to keep up with the power of nature, everything turning and turning. He wished the grindstones were still around, but unlike the rickety wooden wheel, the stones would have fetched a handsome price even in the 70s. He imagined all the pieces of the mill back together again, one functioning body, and he thought of the story the agent had told them about the ghost. One day at the turn of the century, a worker got his sleeve caught in a gear. Warren could see him being pulled along against his will, fighting the machine, a scream, a horrid ripping sound, and the blood. What was grist anyway? What was so valuable about it that it was worth that man's hand? The agent claimed that the man haunted the mill for years.

He noticed that the rubber giraffe was still on the floor and he wondered if maybe he should run after them to give it to Fay. Wouldn't her little face light up with joy at the sight of it? Fergus would be especially pleased. He leaned over to pick it up, then pulled his hand back in fright when it moved. He shook his head and laughed at himself. It was no ghost, although in many ways he wished it was. Paranormal activity was preferable to the reality that the mill had just shifted, perhaps sliding one inch closer to the abyss.

Slogging through the rain suddenly seemed like a sane alternative to staying where he was. He regained his composure and looked around the room, reassuring himself of its normalcy. He'd insisted on keeping the decoration rigorously simple in honor of the build-ing's history, refusing to let Mica soften it up with fruity colors. The walls were white. The objects in the room—the thick-legged tables, the rugged leather chairs, the plain drapes—were proof that he had not allowed his family to succumb to sentimental domesticity.

The building shook again and he stood up. Water was gushing in now along the sills, and he thought, good, maybe that will lessen the forces of the runoff on either side of the house. He wandered into the kitchen to see if they had a mop because he didn't want the old pine boards to warp. But there didn't seem to be any cleaning supplies. Mica had planned to hire a service from town. She said if she was forced to be here, she was not about to spend all her time cleaning it. But look, now there was an emergency and no tools to deal with it. He went back to the living room. A trickle of water had escaped the hearth and was inching its way towards the window, proving that the floor was now tilting towards the gorge. This was bad. The building would have to be shored up when this was over. He hoped that that was all.

There was a sound in the driveway and his heart lifted, thinking they had waved someone down to bring them home. Or maybe they had come back to save him. If that were the case, he would go without protest, not because he really thought the building was going down, but because it would mean so much to them. Maybe it would even serve to bring him and Mica closer. But it was not a car. A massive boulder bounced and slid down from the parking area and plunged into the gorge with a watery crash. He was trying to absorb what had happened when suddenly, as if tied to the boulder, the black Lexus came sliding into view. Warren held his breath and felt his heart race, but the car caught on an exposed root with its own axle just before going over the edge. It seemed secure for now, and he relaxed a little, letting himself get angry with Mica for leaving the car in such a vulnerable position to begin with.

With a lurch, he felt himself trip a few feet across the floor towards the window, which he realized was now slightly canted over the gorge. Hold on, he told the house, hold on. He felt the force of the building straining against the pressures of gravity, torn between the safety of the land and the release of the water. He thought of his family scrambling up the hill. They couldn't have made it that far, not to the road yet, not with the baby and the toddler. He supposed it was just as well they were gone. They'd have ruined his resolve with their irrational fear. This mill was built for the ages, and he and it were going to win this thing. They were going to face it together. There would be glory in merely holding his ground. How many men could claim that?

The heavy beams above began to creak, and maybe that was

a good thing. They were willing to bend rather than break. He looked up and saw that the chandelier had begun to twitch, but that could not be good. His instinct told him to run, but his intellect told him otherwise. He was not a fan of instinct. Humans were not big on hard-wired responses. His was a species that depended on flexibility for survival.

His hand went to his chin. Maybe he could find a dry spot in the hearth for a small fire and heat up some water to shave. He was cold, and he realized he was shaking violently. According to the realtor, the worker had not died when he lost his hand—she did not want Warren to think that someone had bled to death here. No, his colleagues had saved him with quick thinking, and he went on to live a good long life. But the hand had gone through the stones, ruining the day's grain, which had to be sold for pig feed. According to legend, the man returned later, after he died, always searching for his hand, always crying out, forever looking for what he'd lost, trying to be whole once again.

As if by magic, the electricity came back on and Warren wanted to cheer out loud. The bulbs in the chandelier shone through the grimness of the day, illuminating the room. He'd held out and this was his reward. Electricity meant hot water. He could wash up leisurely, revel in the warmth while the storm petered itself out. Then he'd go to find his family. They would be in bad shape somewhere out there, probably huddled under a tree, or if they were lucky, some farmer's old woodshed. The world was a dangerous place and he could not wait to lead them to the safety of the hearth. He put his hand on the back of a chair to balance himself. The floor had become unpredictable, and he advanced across the room, steadying himself on one solid object then another. The chandelier continued to sway, and because it was lit up now, it cast odd moving shadows across the room. As if shoved by an invisible hand, the coffee table slid a few inches and banged against him, knocking him to his knees. He struggled to his feet, and stood still for a moment to regain his composure. He felt as if something was very wrong, but it was all right because he was almost there, and he smiled. His family would be so happy, so surprised when they saw him, clean-shaven and relaxed, looking like a winner. Jason would realize that the old man knew what he was about. Mica would look at him with love in her eyes. The beam above buckled with a horrific noise, then, just as quickly as it had come on, the lights went out again.

Better to sit for now. Too dark, too dark, too loud. He found a heavy chair, not where it should be, not where it should be at all, and at a peculiar angle, but as he sank into the welcoming leather he felt the tension seep from his body. This was the thing. His fears shall not be in the way. He would wait it out, right here, and let history wash over him, his home, his hearth, over and over, floating over the chaos of his life like a blessing.

Woodbine & Asters

THE STREAM IS full from the storm last night, the storm that stripped the trees bare, making the blue sky bigger in one fell swoop. Now those leaves are clogging the water with orange dams and red dams, breaking up and building again. Nedra and I sit soaking in the sun on the mossy two-plank footbridge, looking down at the stream rushing along in tics and shrugs while those two kids from next door squat in the willow tree a few feet away, gaping. Mattie and Wink are hoping we'll get bored with just sitting and go hang with them but they are wrong. Wrong, wrong, wrong. Willow leaves flutter goodbye as the branch sinks into the water, pressed down by the boys' weight.

"Looks like fingers dipping in the stream," Nedra says. "A long delicate hand testing the temperature, getting ready for a bath."

Fingers. I don't know about that girl. All pleased, she runs her own fingers through her tight peachy curls. Yes, peachy. She's a peculiar color that one, what I call sallow and she calls tawny like she's a lioness. But tall? Nedra's legs dangle so far her toes touch the water, which she flicks up at the boys just because she can and doesn't mind the ice-coldness. I'd slip off the plank trying and that makes me steam. I'll never be that tall, not even when I'm fifteen like Nedra is now. I'm a mature thirteen say my parents, but that won't give me more height because they are short people themselves, and they know it.

Besides, the branch doesn't look like fingers at all. I would call it one wild head of hair, like my grandmother's in the morning before she braids it into a long rope down her back, a rope that used to be silky black but now is as tweedy as my father's jacket. Esther is young for a grandmother, but she is my own mother's mother after all, so the gray is not before its time. Esther is not Nedra's grandmother though. Nedra is her foster child so I don't know what that makes them. Or us.

Esther is on the screened back porch, far enough away so she can't hear us, but close enough so that we can hear her yell, which she does twice telling the boys to not break that branch or they'll have to deal with her wrath. They stop bouncing and then forget and start again, not meaning to disobey just being young and stupid and Esther knows that. She was holding their mom's hand tight when they popped into the world one after another all wet and screaming. Right in their own purple house down on Harmony! I made Wink show me the bed. His mom asked if I wanted to see the pictures and I said no. No thank you.

I was born at St. Stephen's Lying-In in the city, in a delivery room like any normal child, but like the boys, Nedra is another story. She was the last baby "birthed" at Sacred Oak, the old commune up in the mountains, sometime after Esther had already pulled anchor saying it was too much work working together. She had lived there as a single mom when it first started way back when, before they even called them "single moms" says my father, but called them something else. It's where Mom was a kid, and ran feral according to my father. He had a regular life growing up, as we do now, and he worries about me when I go to visit Esther, which is about as often as I can, not just summers but even now on long weekends.

My father told me that Nedra's birth mom showed up at Sacred Oak already in labor, and then left empty-armed and flat-stomached the minute after. Nedra says it wasn't like that at all, but won't tell me what it was like. Sometimes she takes my hand and says how happy she is to have a sister, which is what we have sometimes made-believed even though we're not really blood. Esther says nothing, except to say that we all come from the same place. Her answers are sometimes not very satisfying with specific information.

Whatever the story was, Sacred Oak soon fell apart under "its own dead weight of consensus," as my father calls it, and there was baby Nedra needing a home. Esther took her and the state seemed happy enough to leave the situation as it stood. And here she's been.

And here we are.

Today is elderberry day. It's dark like a cave behind the porch screen but I can feel Esther's wide olive eyes on us while she bottles the juice, juice that will turn magically into wine someday. She says we'll all drink it at my wedding or at the birth of my firstborn whatever comes first but don't tell my parents that. Her copper funnel aims the rubyness into thin glass necks, same as in spring when it steers goat milk from bucket to jar, or in summer when it's shot red from juiced tomatoes, or winter when it glazes over from the maple syrup she taps from her own woods that begin right here at the footbridge and run to the top of Freedom Hill. It's truly Esther's woods for a whole half-mile chunk, on paper as well as in her heart, and in deer season she stands out there and tells the hunters so "in no uncertain terms," as Nedra says, but only because she has heard Esther say those words.

The two dogs under Esther's worktable whimper in their high pitch but they are such odd ducks I don't think of it. They have a little bit of every breed says Esther, so they are extra sensitive to universal vibes. But I think they are only dim and can't tell the difference between an intruder and the wind. Then Esther says "Damn it to hell" loud as if she's yelling at the boys but still I don't look up thinking she's only spilled. The dogs start barking in their odd ducky way with every yelp ending with a question mark.

Nedra jerks around like the lead goat does when it hears me

coming, but she doesn't even look at the dogs who are now scratching at the screen to get out, but eyes 378, the county road that runs up the side of the woods. The road only has a number. Esther says that's how much imagination the government has that all it can come up with is 378 for such a lovely road which should be named aster or woodbine or goldenrod for the plants that grow along its banks, as if it was a winding river. Now I hear a big rumbling coming down that road deafening as the storm last night and soon we all see what the whimpering and cursing is about. Some ominous vehicle is hoving down on the farm stand.

Even though the house seems circled by trees, Esther can still spot her stand on 378 from the back porch. She keeps a path clear, a path wide enough for the cart, too narrow for a car, and even from the kitchen we can hear if a customer clangs the bell for service. If I take a running jump off the back steps, down the lawn, across the footbridge, and through that snippet of the woods to the farm stand, I can make it there in seventy seconds, even though I alarm the customers with my gasping and heaving. Esther tells me not to knock myself out like that, her customers are cool and can be trusted. But that's no way to run a business my father says, and anyway, I like to make change and use the scale and pretend that I live here always and not just visiting.

So we watch or bark or say damn as the big yellow flatbed pulls over, and on that sits a bulldozer bigger than Esther's farm stand, which is lost in the shadow. Right away I know the two guys in the flatbed are not here to buy pumpkins or a sack of dusty potatoes.

"I want to go look," yells Wink, standing on one branch and holding on above to another bouncing up and down making the whole tree alive with its branchy hand slapping the water.

"I want to look too," screams Mattie, the words pumping out of him with every bounce.

"You stay right where you are," Nedra says to the boys, bossing as if she were a grown-up even though she's not all that much older than me. At home I'm the oldest, the one calling the shots.

"What do those guys want?" I ask as if I don't already know they're here to modernize old 378 in spite of Esther saying no. I turn to look back up at the porch in time to see the funnel hit the screen and this is not good, not good at all. Nedra gives my leg a slap and starts to put her socks and sneakers back on, so I do too.

A big man in mustard coveralls is climbing down from his rig, and I can't see who gets out of the other side. "I don't think they're parked on the asters," I say to Nedra trying to comfort because she has her yellow-brown eyes narrowed and I don't need both Esther and Nedra storming around for the rest of the weekend complaining about the sorry-ass state of the world.

"Dead flowers are the least of our problems," says Nedra tying her laces into a tight double knot. The flatbed spews diesel smoke that has begun to drift like a low black cloud up the path towards us and I get really pissed when she says things like "the least of our problems" because those are words of Esther's and Nedra has no right to them.

"Pricks!" says Esther, as she comes stomping down off the steps, letting the porch door slam behind like a gunshot, the two mutts a yelping blur ahead of her. Nedra and I find ourselves in the way, so we jump aside and my sneakers aren't even tied yet. The frantic dogs dash past us almost knocking us down, and then Esther clomps by in her winter workboots which all by themselves look as if they mean business. We follow her thick braid swinging back and forth like a bullwhip and I think she's not going to stop at all but continue on over the mustard-suit man, who has foolishly wandered up the path. When Esther does stop it is with no notice and the man has to take one step back for a buffer. He's puffing as if he'd been walking for miles instead of just a few feet, and his lipless mouth is stretched in a smile that shows all his metal fillings.

"Good morning," Esther says, and smiles that tight grin of hers she uses on the hunters when she chases them away.

"Yes good morning," he says, his eyes darting around because that particular look of Esther's is hard to take. "Sweet place you've got here, all the animals, the kids." He looks at me and raises his hand in a little wave so I smile because it is rude not to but Nedra gives me the hairy eyeball so I look down at my feet and become interested in a splintered hunk of wood instead and wonder when's a good time to bend over to do my laces. "We thought we'd get a little clearing done this fall to let the ground settle so road construction can get under way early spring. None of the big trees. Just the scrubby stuff along the verge. We'll try not to be too much in your way, Ma'am..."

"Damn straight you won't." Esther pulls her pouch of tobacco out of her plaid shirt pocket, still smiling. Nedra folds her arms and hugs them as if she were afraid one is going to fly up and do some damage.

The guy looks completely away from Esther now and I don't blame him because even I start looking around as if I've never seen the place before. He nods like a pecking chicken at the goat shed, the hen house, the pony paddock, the compost bins, the orchard, and the vegetable garden that runs all the way past the house to the stream, a garden that we pulled wine-colored beets from just this morning.

Esther has been rolling a smoke this whole time, her hands all stained elderberry, making the cigarette paper bruised. She licks the glue just as the man's eyes return to hers so that she has both hands up to her mouth like the barn cat ready to pounce and her eyes look golden-green in the filtered light. "Get off my property," she says. "And you can tell the state that we like the road just as it is."

He opens his mouth but nothing comes out, so he turns and heads back to the flatbed, where there is another guy in jeans messing with the bulldozer. The dogs start to follow him but think better of it and decide to sit at Esther's feet instead and drool on her boots.

I hear the willow shaking dryly behind me and the boys laughing in the branches. I look at Nedra because I want to go back to the house, but like Esther, she is not taking her eyes off the man's wide mustard back, so we can do nothing but stand there.

Much too soon both men return, the other man with a cell phone in one hand and a map rolled up in the other like he's about to hit one of the dogs, but he's smiling like he just won the lottery, and it worries me all this smiling for no good reason. "Good morning girls," he says to me and Nedra, who bows her head like a queen and I don't dare do anything. "Boys," he shouts, and waves over at the tree, which shakes furiously. He faces Esther directly. "This road improvement has been in the works for years now, Ma'am. Hearings, zoning board meetings, everything. It's been approved. We're just doing our job."

"Sounds to me as if you need more straightening than the road." There is no more Esther smile. "A community action suit has been filed to prevent the state from splitting this town down the middle with a highway, and nothing can be done until that's settled." She taps her cigarette on the back of her hand.

"How come he's still smiling?" I whisper to Nedra. I know I must be missing something, because no one smiles when Esther gets mad.

"He's not," she whispers back. "His mouth just hasn't caught up with the rest of him yet."

I hold my hand up and block out the bottom half of his face, and sure enough, without his mouth, he's not smiling at all.

"We're not doing road work today," says mustard-suit man. "The state always has rights of way to clear foliage."

"Up to twenty feet on either side, Ma'am," says the jeans guy, unrolling his map so at least I know he can't hit anyone with it anymore. "Let me show you something. You can see how your farm stand has always been in violation, sitting in our right of way, how the wider road won't allow for such a big shoulder anymore. That's why we've offered to move your stand to just around the corner, over on Harmony. Good visibility, easy parking." He finally looks up from the blue lines on the paper to Esther, his smile gone, his mouth now at home with his eyes. "There shouldn't be any problem."

"You're right," Esther says. "There won't be any problem at all."

"High traffic's a good thing for your business," mustard-suit man says, trying to make nice and I wonder if he's afraid of the guy with the map. "An improved road brings new homes, new business, new money. More people buying vegetables. Think about it."

"I have," says Esther. "And there's no one going so hungry or cold here that we need to sell out our town."

Actually, my toes have gone numb with cold from standing in the damp woods for so long, and right before the truck showed up I was thinking about going into the kitchen to see if there was any more apple pie left from breakfast, but then Nedra shouts out

"That's right!" as if this was some revival meeting. So I nod like I'm agreeing with her, but I'm thinking that it wouldn't do either of them any harm to have a few more customers. What the state gives for foster kids is not even enough to keep a cat alive says Mom.

All of a sudden Esther whips around to go back to the house and that braid of hers which is as thick as my wrist goes airborne whacking the map. The man gives Esther a look behind her back, and almost says something, but there is Nedra leaning towards him scowling like I see her practice in the mirror sometimes, her peachy eyebrows deeply angled down her nose. She looks as if she's been waiting her whole life for some dunderhead like himself to wander into her life. He flaps one hand at the air and turns away.

Nedra turns too, and twitches her head for us to move on. We go back across the slippery footbridge and I can hear the men shuffle through the wet leaves. They are mumbling to one another but the only word I can make out for sure is "bitch."

Esther and the dogs have gone into the house, slamming the door behind her so hard it bounces open again and we won't go near it. Nedra stops at the willow tree and runs her hand down a branch, stripping it to a whip. Wink and Mattie look down on us like a couple of baboons.

"What's going to happen? What's going to happen?" they ask, and are all excited and I know they want to go closer to the bulldozer but don't dare.

"Oh shut up," I tell them.

"Esther says no one's allowed to say shut up here," says Mattie.

"I'm telling," says Wink.

"All of you hush," says Nedra, and she throws a look to the house.

Esther comes out, leaving the screen door open again, and I worry that the nasty yellow jackets will drown in the elderberry juice and ruin my wedding wine. The stupid dogs jump about her as she comes down the lawn holding a plain white envelope.

"Go give this to Jared, boys. He must be in his shop because he doesn't answer the phone."

Mattie and Wink leap down as one, landing hard on four sneakered feet, slipping on the wet mint underneath and almost sliding into the stream before they get their bearings and head off home hooting and whooping. Jared is their dad and he's a lawyer, even though he doesn't really do that as far as I can tell, not like lawyer friends of my father's who wear dark suits and talk in life-or-death voices. Jared has a braid almost as long as Esther's, and he works on an old typewriter from his kitchen table when he isn't building furniture in the garage, and when their mom doesn't need the table herself for laying out clothes patterns. Before Mom met my father, she used to date Jared, although she says date is not exactly what you called it then. This was when she still lived with Esther at the commune, before Jared got a scholarship to Princeton and left, before he met Moira and brought her back here to have babies in his bed. My father shakes his head and says what a waste of a good education.

When the boys are gone, Esther looks at me and twists her mouth into a smile before she walks back to the house and slumps down on the porch steps. She turns and leans on her elbow, reaching up to shut the door and I'm glad she remembered about the yellow jackets and the elderberry. Nedra sits next to Esther and leans up against one shoulder, and I lean up against the other. All the animals are quiet for once, not even the dogs at Esther's feet are moving, not scratching or licking themselves although every time they take a breath they wheeze. She lights her smoke and the smell is sweet and damp like the floor of the woods. Mom says it's a disgusting habit, but Esther says it's okay if you roll your own and not those filtered sticks full of chemicals, which are too convenient already rolled in their slick little boxes. I think Esther is right, but I don't tell that to Mom.

From the road comes the sounds of creaking and groaning and metal crunching on metal as the bed slowly lifts up to dump the bulldozer on the ground. If I close my eyes it sounds like garbage collection day, but there is no collection this far out in the country. There is just the dump. I'm thinking I'd like to go on a dump adventure this afternoon with Nedra and see what we can surprise Esther with to cheer her up, but when I turn to Nedra she is looking into Esther's eyes as if they don't even need words, the smoke from the cigarette wrapping like a ribbon around them.

That burns me. It's *my* grandmother. I start to steam, not just at Nedra but at her mother too who had some nerve leaving baby Nedra behind where Esther could just scoop her up. I bend over to fix my laces and my face feels so hot and red I can't even tie right, and I feel stupid being so mad. It's Nedra who should be angry at her real mom, not me. She should be off fuming someplace and leave me with Esther to myself.

I sit up with a start when the earth shudders. The bulldozer has finally slipped off the flatbed.

"Pigs," mutters Esther.

"Two little pigs," says Nedra. "Huffing and puffing like wolves."

Esther takes a long drag off her smoke and exhales slowly. "I remember when I first saw this place," she says. Nedra sits right up and I lean in close. We love when she talks about those times before Mom was born. Even my father says that I could learn a bit of history from Esther, just don't romanticize it, but since Esther never talks about the romantic part where she's knocked up, there's no problem. "We had just returned from a month of registering voters and the bunch of us camped out here in the woods for a week before we went back to school. There was nothing here then, it was so calm, especially after months of people hating one another like it was a contest. Even our own government against us, using clubs, hoses, chains, anything. They weren't accountable to anyone."

"But to God and their own conscience," says Nedra.

Word thief I think to myself. Later I will tell Nedra to go find her own words and leave Esther's alone.

"They didn't have to answer to anyone in this world at any rate," says Esther. "But we always owned the high moral road." She exhaled a string of rings that dissolved one at a time above us. "A few years later when I left school, this was the only place I wanted to be. We were going to do it differently here." She paused, looking down the path, but she's not seeing the truck and the men and the bulldozer. No, she's seeing farther than that, she's seeing as far as she once did from that old time looking to now, except she was expecting now to be different than it appears to be. She lifts up one side of her mouth in a twisted smile and snuffs the cigarette out in the dirt and puts the butt in her shirt pocket. "I still like to think of old 378 as the high moral road," she says at last.

The mustard guy climbs into the bulldozer, and it starts up with a few grunts. When it suddenly jolts from a stutter to a roar the dogs stand up and circle, waiting for a cue from Esther. She is up now too, shielding her eyes and looking over at Harmony for the boys.

"My father says that the drive from the city will be quicker when they improve the road," I say meekly as if it were a consolation prize.

Esther smiles a little, but not in her eyes, and she reaches down to brush the hair back from my face. Her hand smells like tobacco and elderberry. "I'm not sure the state's intentions are to develop a faster delivery system of sweet Alice Rose."

"He says this place will be worth more," I say. "That's good, right?"

Esther coughs so hard she has to stamp her foot. "Depends what your definition of worth is. It doesn't mean a fig unless I sell it, and then what? I'll have money and not what means the most to me. That's what selling out means, girls."

"Traitors are worse than the enemy itself," says Nedra and spits on the ground.

You'd think this kid went to a military academy the way she talks, instead of the co-op school in the valley. I hear this stuff too, when Esther's friends from the University come around, when they talk the way they do and shake their heads. But I don't repeat things as if they were my own. There's no time to get all worked up again about the word thief because the bulldozer begins scraping its way along the edge of the road. A horrible noise it makes as it begins to grind back the brush into mangled piles, upending and tearing the bushes, and exposing the roots.

"They're not going to hurt the maples," I say, raising my voice until it cracks. "And the other stuff will grow back."

Esther paces, going to the corner of the house to check if the boys are coming and then back to the other corner of the house to look at the bulldozer on 378, and every time she turns around she bumps into one or the other of the dogs who are at her heels. We just sit there looking at her, our heads going back and forth like we're at a tennis match. The geese start honking so Nedra and I stand up. The geese always make a commotion when they see people on Harmony, as if they own it and sure enough Mattie and Wink come lunging across the front lawn waving a note. The dogs go running to meet them but not Esther. She looks behind them. I can tell she was expecting Jared, not some piece of paper and I hope this doesn't mean trouble on top of trouble. The boys stand panting in front of her and the dogs sit panting looking up at her and we wait at her back. She takes the note and reads it to herself first, then out loud over the thick rumbling of the bulldozer.

"Esther, I don't see what I can do other than file the suit which I've already done. To tell you the truth, the law is on their side, right or wrong. It is what it is. We can't be martyrs about this. Jared."

"Jared couldn't have written that," says Nedra who has been reading over Esther's shoulders, which is the advantage of the very tall. She turns to the boys. "Are you sure you gave him Esther's note?" They nod and back up a step.

"Mom says he can't come running over here every time Esther smells a gross injustice," Wink says, and the word "gross" lingers on his lips.

"He's busy," says Mattie. "Mom told him no more pro bono until all the bills are paid."

They are word thieves too, repeating exactly what their mom said, the same mom who squeezed the two of them into the world on her bed with Esther by her side. The same mom who probably didn't expect for them to steal her words and spend them here in front of Esther. Nedra takes three long steps towards them, so they turn and run down to the stream. The dogs are snapping at their heels thinking they're playing and Nedra stops to pick up a rock. She throws too late, the boys have already crossed the plank, heading to where the bulldozer inches along the woods, snipping at edges as if it were just giving a hair cut. I'd like to have a closer look myself but I know that is out of the question.

"The boys are still on your land, Esther," Nedra says. "Should I run them back where they came from?"

Esther slowly crumples up Jared's note with both hands, twisting it into a hard knot. "They're just children."

We continue to stand there because it's impossible to take our eyes off the sight and sound of the bulldozer's progress along the roadside. Roots ripping, branches snapping, birds squawking high above. It's horrible, I know, but not the end of the world. There will still be plenty left when they are done, still maple trees for her to tap in January and boil down in her iron cauldron over an open fire so we can have syrup for our pancakes all year round. But I don't say any of that. I hear the bulldozer grinding and struggling as it gets mired in places because the ground is soupy from last night's rain.

"Maybe they'll get stuck and won't be able to go any farther," I say loudly and it's the first thing that's been said for so long that both Nedra and Esther are startled and look at me.

"They won't get stuck, Alice Rose," Esther says over the sound, and then she starts to smile. This is no good, I think, this smile. "But what if they came across something that couldn't be rolled over?" she says directly to Nedra.

With deep dread I know exactly what she's thinking, and of course so does Nedra, who says it first and with enthusiasm. "Passive resistance!"

The next thing I know there are Nedra and Esther heading towards the woods, the dogs so excited they almost skid off the plank following them. We are going to meet the bulldozer head-on and I try to keep up even though I'd rather not. Nedra is always accusing me of what she calls conflict avoidance, but it's only that I hate fights. There is so much noise they can't hear me say slow down.

"You just bear witness girls," Esther shouts. "I don't want you getting involved in this."

"No," says Nedra. "I'm going limp with you."

The two of them start arguing but I can't hear from the racket as we get closer and there is a buzzing noise in my head. The mustard-suit guy in the driver's seat sees Esther and Nedra and tries to wave them off but only slows, and does not brake. The guy in jeans comes running from the road still clutching his map and phone and I see his mouth shape words at Esther as she is lying down, "What the hell are you doing?" and he might as well have snatched them out of my own mouth. Esther is settling herself directly in the path of the bulldozer not ten yards from the blade. The dogs are beside themselves not knowing what to do but jump and yelp at her.

Through all this she is still arguing with Nedra and pointing for her to stand with me, neither of them really paying any attention to the bulldozer. I see the blade drop into the wet dirt and I run to Esther.

"No!" There is a terrible pounding in my head, a thick pressure against my skull that I think will never escape and the "no" echoes in the woods because just then the bulldozer stops with a lurch. The mustard guy has killed the engine. Esther gives in now and says that Nedra can lie with her, but only her feet can be directly in front of the blade. I stand shaking over them as they arrange themselves on the damp ground, making a line head to toe, Nedra's boots resting on Esther's braid in the mud. The dogs start pawing the disturbed earth.

Mattie and Wink come whooping from the flatbed where they'd been toying, and they scramble up the blade of the bulldozer just as mustard-suit man climbs down from the seat, and the boys finally possess the thing they have been so in awe of. The map guy and mustard-suit man are both screaming at the same time, one of them shouting into his phone and waving his free hand in the air. I can't listen because I am afraid for Esther and Nedra so the only words I hear are "crazy bitch," and those might very well be the only words they're saying.

"Don't do this Esther," I say. "The farm stand can go on Harmony. The rest of these woods will be okay."

"Until when?" she says.

"The roots will bear us up," says Nedra, not looking at me but gazing up at the leafless blue, that look she gets when she starts making things in her mind that are not real and never will be. "We are a bridge, plank touching plank, stretching our limbs for justice."

"Shut up, shut up!" I scream. "You don't know what those words even are, you stole them, you thief!"

They both look up at me in shock although no one is more surprised than me. Esther murmurs my name but then I hear a police siren wail off in the distance. I have tears in my eyes because I'm as ripped up as the forest floor. I want to lie down with Esther and have her be proud of me and I don't want to give Nedra the satisfaction of being the only one with Esther, the one on the high moral plane down there in the dirt. But someone has to stay upright. One of us has to be free to run back to the house and call my father.

Location! Location! 18+ acres of remote land with everything you could ask for if you love the Outdoors! 1500+ ft. of Stream frontage, Snowmobiling trails. Good hunting. Southern Exposure and Privacy!

A fact: Adam is not my original name, but that other one wasn't very lucky. I chose Adam because it is powerful, with four letters like the pillars of a house. Not only that, Adam was first in the Bible and I am the first here. Almost. Others have been here before me. I know this by the black circle on the ground where they built a fire right there, there where I have cleared the thicket, where the three trees are fallen and dead. I know they were hunters because of what they left behind. I am very good at understanding the world by studying the facts because I know that only facts can lead to the heart of a mystery. Like these rocks. They are black on one side only, the side that once faced the fire to keep the flames in the circle so the hunters could keep warm by the heat and not die from it. And to not die even more they slept inside tents while the fire kept on burning outside to frighten the animals and keep them away. Which was smart of the hunters because tents don't keep much of anything out. You can rip them with your hands once you get a tear started. I have a tent I made myself but soon I am going to have a cabin with real corners. I'm going to make logs with the hatchet the hunters left and Chop! Chop! until the trees are made into logs and I will notch them and stack them in exact forty-five degree angles to one another. My cabin will be over the spot where I have already begun to dig. The cabin will be my entrance to the underground where it's safe.

But first I need to study the facts in the Farmer's Almanac to see when is a good time to start building dwellings. I keep the book in a plastic bread bag under a piece of tent because it is that important but before I take it out for the day I must wash my hands in the stream and rub at the cracks between the fingers. There is not much to be done about the perma-dirt under the nails though, and when I go into town I make my hands into fists so no one can see. I dry my hands on my pants but that has made my palms dirty again so I start over and this time I just hold my hands up to the sun to dry. This gets my face all hot and sleepy and I close my eyes and the world inside my head turns yellow with floating red splotches. Those are the colors of the Almanac too and that is no coincidence. The Almanac was written by Robert B. Thomas in 1792 but this is what I think: I think it is knowledge handed down over thousands of years through a secret society and this Robert B. Thomas decided he'd make some money and sell that information to whoever. Everyone wants to sell what they have in the end. They would sell the earth right out from under them. I hate that about people. They want more money to buy more things but there is no happiness in things. "You've got more than enough," as Grandpa used to say. The happiness is inside and the more you can do to let the inside out the better. That is what I want to do with my life. Help people look at the inside of things.

When my hands are dry I remove the book, carefully, carefully, because it has gotten a little ragged living here with me in the hole. There are facts on the pages—what days are good for fishing or planting or destroying pests—that have already been calculated and are printed for anyone to read. But if you know numbers like I do, and if you know so much you have figured out Robert B. Thomas's secret formula, then you know more than the others. You know what's underneath. As Robert B. Thomas says, the universe can be understood by the numbers. Numbers can explain the meaning of life and what we're doing here and what our mission is. By carefully studying "deviations from the normal" I know I am to build a cabin over my safe home in the ground, and if I keep working at these calculations they will tell me when to start helping people and how.

I don't need math for some things though, like when is a good day to start work on dwellings. The Timetable doesn't list "start work on dwellings" exactly but it does list "good for starting projects" and that's what this is, a woodworking project just like in Shop. But bad news. It says here on page 229 that there are only two days in June for starting projects, and they are at the end of the month, so I have to wait. There are good days for "logging," but they were last week. The only thing good today is "slaughter livestock."

You can't go against the numbers. Robert B. Thomas writes that there is "a cause and effect pattern to all phenomena." I had to look up "phenomena" at the library because I'm not so good at words as I am at numbers, so I tore the page out of the Dictionary and now I keep it folded in the Almanac so I don't forget. It says a phenomena is "any fact that is apparent to the senses and can be scientifically described." Which means the whole world is phenomenal because I can describe it all by studying the facts. Like the black snake on the pants this morning. The pants are in a ball behind the Tree of Mushrooms, and they are bright orange. That is one of the facts I examined to determine that the others who were here before me were hunters, even though they forgot the pants so long ago that they are not so bright anymore and have been shredded by mice. Now a strange gray family of bugs lives underneath, eating away at the cloth. All that will be left one day is a zipper, like a little silver spine. I could not catch the snake to see what was inside of him, but I'm sure he was full of gray bugs. It is all a cycle. The Almanac is all about cycles. Sunspots have eleven-year cycles. The sunspots are an important phenomena only I can't examine them with my naked eyes or I will go blind. I have to study them from the photograph in the Almanac which makes the sun look like a giant circle of ash, just like the one the hunters left here on the ground. The Almanac says that "compared to most stars, the Sun is fairly stable," but like everything else, it goes through cycles and is more active now than it has been in the last 8000 years. 8000. 8000. 8000. All those zeros after an eight—the symbol for infinity. That means something infinitely huge is coming. That is why I am here and not where I used to be. Robert B. Thomas says nothing in the universe happens haphazardly. Nothing. A fact: Creatures hide in the underbrush all around me, darting behind trees, and small shapes flit above from limb to limb, but these movements have a pattern and if I study them long enough the pattern will reveal itself. There is no such thing as chaos, no matter how chaotic it gets. Robert B. Thomas says that none of us have *as yet* gained sufficient insight into the mysteries of the universe but I think I have come very close.

"Your body is your temple," Grandma used to say when she slapped me and now I see. The leaves of the trees make a dome above me and the trunks are pillars, like a temple. My temple. My body is this clearing. Grandma wanted me to find this place and make it mine. But what if the trees hate the roots that imprison them? What if the trunks are tired of standing all the time? What if they want to bend?

A chipmunk sneaks out from under the rotting log. "Go away!" I shout and he goes back under the log. So much goes on where we can't see, but it is just as real there as here, if not more so. As the log is the gateway for the burrow, so will my cabin be the gateway to my real home underneath, closer to the "phenomena" of geothermal warmth from the core that will keep me warm in winter. Some energy comes from above, like the sun, but some energy comes from below. Then there is the energy that comes from within. We are all our own systems unto ourselves, and we too can be understood. You just have to know what energy to tap into at any given time. You also have to be careful not to interfere with that energy. For instance: On page 190, Robert B. Thomas talks about the dangers of "bio-aerosols," like dandruff and dead skin cells and fur particles that affect global warming, which can lead to other bad things like the cooling of the geothermal warmth under my cabin. So I wear a black wool cap and I do not scratch my skin. Every few days I lie down in the icy stream in my clothes and cap and look up at the branches and hold my breath until I'm clean again. The hunters were not so careful. The hunters released fur particles and dead deer cells into the atmosphere, so I will have to dig very deep. It is time to get the hatchet out. Another thing about the Almanac: It is very important to keep track of what day it is, because you must know when a month is over and it is time to start fresh again. Not at zero though. There is no absolute zero.

Today might be good for slaughtering livestock, but that does not mean I will. For one thing, I only have the chipmunk and I have scared him away. So today, like all the days—except some really, really bad ones—I will dig at my hole with the hatchet, chopping away at the dark soil, cutting through roots thick as fingers and prying out head-sized rocks. It is hard work. The hatchet is dull and that might be why the hunters left it. People hate dull. I would be a better digger if I had the right tool. The animals have everything they need to survive at birth, but not us. "Useless," as Grandpa used to say, and shake his head. I have to do everything with the hatchet because it is all I have, even though I hate when the metal scrapes against rock or bone. That sound goes right through me. It is work to open a can with a hatchet, so a can opener is one of the things I have to find the next time I hitch into town. I wish the hunters had left a shovel, but why would hunters have shovels? They don't bury what they kill. The dead deer still lies by the stream, through all these seasons. We grow old together, the deer and I.

While I have the book open, I go over the day's calculations again, because there was something that keeps it from being a lucky powerful day. Some days I have to think extra hard, so hard that shapes start moving and get fuzzy, and the forest turns a peculiar color, and sparks of light shoot like glass from the sky. That's when

I forget about the tables and charts and concentrate on the advertisements to calm my head. The ads are a different part of the same master puzzle, but easier on the brain. On page five, a mattress company mentions NASA. Why? The answer is all the way on page 194 where the Almanac explains how it bases "normal" on thirty-year statistical averages prepared by government meteorological agencies. So by dropping NASA into the equation, the mattress people are saying, look, this mattress is completely normal. But what does any agency know about normal? Nothing. They know nothing about normal.

On page eleven is an ad with small brown birds on a wire. Feathers can sometimes brush away bad luck, so I keep three sparrow feathers tucked in the Almanac. None from the crows though. A crow overhead is a black force waiting to overtake my soul. I worry about the crows. They were at the stream to drink this morning and, as always, they took a few pokes at the deer, even though he can provide nothing for them anymore. I tried to count the crows, but they were changing numbers too quickly and I couldn't keep track. First three, then five, then two flew away only to come back as a foursome, and then there were more, then less, and I couldn't calculate fast enough. Animals are closer to nature, and they don't need secret formulas like we do. They get their information from the universe and "phenomena" without any calculation at all. They live by voices we cannot hear. If I stay here in the woods for a long time maybe I will become more like the animals and less like the humans. Humans have not been very lucky for me. And most have very bad numbers. Robert B. Thomas says the Golden Number is twelve, but not for me. One and two is me and two more, and that would not be golden. They always come in twos. A terrible number. That is why I needed to get away. I have to discover more meanings.

It is time to put the Almanac back in its bread bag for the day while I work, but then I see the bag is ripped, so I hold on to it and think. I need more plastic in my life. When I go to town next I will get some more bags from the dumpster, and then I will go to the bank to find out how tall I am. At the bank door is a height chart, so the teller can tell the police how tall a robber is when he's leaving with all the money. That's what Grandma told me when she brought me to the bank to hide her egg money from "that bastard." But if it is so safe, I wanted to ask her, why do they need a chart by the door to measure their thieves? I never asked, because she didn't like questions, so it is still a mystery. My height will no longer be a mystery though, if I lean against the chart and ask someone to read the number at my head. I will have to do this without attracting any attention. "Keep your ugly mug down," Grandpa always said as we walked through town. But the danger will be worth the risk, because my height is a number I can use to build my cabin. My own body as a measuring device. One Adam wide, two Adams long, an Adam and a half tall. One day, there could even be a metric conversion for Adams on the Table of Measures.

It is hard to measure some things though. I can measure my height, but not my sadness. It goes very deep. It is very dark. Sometimes when I sit and think I lose track of time, I lose days, and I know afterwards I have been in that dark place. But there's no getting out of that shrinking world until the numbers work. Which can take a long time if you do it right. Do something wrong and it's bad luck for everyone. Like the deer by the stream. It has no head. It cannot be saved. Grandma told me that Jesus Christ was man's savior, which means He did not die to save deer, only men. But that does not mean the deer's life had no meaning. I am trying to find that meaning.

The facts are these: Hunters killed the deer and left it behind a long time ago. All they wanted was the head, and not even all of that, and that was wrong. You have to accept the entire being. "Take me as I am or leave me," Grandpa said to Grandma, before she left. Then he was gone too. First drunk, then dead, then buried. Boom, boom, boom. I was a grandson then, but I am nothing now. Things turned unlucky for me after that, even my original name no longer worked for me. But I have learned to accept the deer the way he is. The carcass is so old and stiff it hardly stinks, just a little when I pry it open once in a while to have a look around. It takes work to get inside when it is all dried up and rubbery. Other animals have eaten some of the body and now they carry the deer inside of them. One animal chewed off an entire leg and took it away. Maybe that leg was used to feed a bear cub and someday it will grow up and eat the hunters. It is all a cycle.

Some cycles are bad. Some cycles make me cry. When I first found the carcass there was still snow on the ground. What was left of the deer was frozen and very flat and I remember thinking that's how I feel sometimes too, so immediately I felt very close to the deer, like we were brothers, only one of us was dead. The belly had been long ago ripped open and the fresh parts removed. But I knew the most important piece was hidden deep in its cage of bone, so I looked for it. The deer used to have a warm, pulsing center, as I do now. I pried and I pulled at the tight old muscle, looking for it, and all I had was this dull hatchet. But it was a powerful day. The numbers were very, very lucky. I base all my calculations on those numbers. I found the heart because I saw the arrow pointing the way. Only I didn't know it was an arrow at first. At first I thought it was just a stick that had worked its way into the flesh, but then I examined it very closely and realized, no, the hunters put this here. Then I could see that they tried to get it back because the shaft was snapped off at the skin. They killed the deer with an arrow and then didn't even want to let it keep it. But the deer kept the arrowhead anyway, and even a little bit of the shaft. A secret. I cut away at everything around it, where the tendons and cartilage had shrunk, and I separated the black flesh from the arrow shaft and the dried heart. I am a good caretaker of the heart. As the months go by it continues to shrink, and I can see the metal points of the arrowhead starting to push through. When it rains I hold it by the piece of shaft and we sit together under my tent. The water comes, but we are safe. I love the dead deer, and I will miss it when it is only a pile of clean, dry bones. Even those won't stay forever. It was a male. I saw the place where the sacs used to be and I have decided they must be good to eat because they were gone first. The head was gone when I found it too, but the head is not chewy. The head cannot be eaten. The hunters took the antlers because they wanted to steal the deer's power so they cut off the head at the top of the neck. The cut is very ragged so they must have used this dull hatchet. Then they whacked the antlers off the head. I can tell by the old yellow bits of jaw and teeth by the flat rock. The flies must have been very fierce. The fresh body would have been covered in flies, laying eggs in the flesh, making the deer alive with maggots. But even the maggots are finished with it now. Some people think maggots are nasty, but if there were no maggots, we would be smothered by the weight of the dead. Cadaver-eaters are part of the cycle. Underneath the deer is a different family of gray bugs helping the body return to the earth. Another part of the cycle. I worry that Grandpa won't be part of the cycle for a long time because the last time I saw him he was in a tight metal box. A suggestion: Don't ever try to drag a body out of a funeral home alone. That is how the Agency will find you.

Another fact: The deer was killed at the stream while he was drinking. On the African savannah, animals call a truce at the watering hole, but not humans. Humans have no rules except those they make up themselves to serve themselves. "Because I said so," as Grandpa used to say. When I am thinking, sometimes I think about the deer's broken head, the way the hunters left with the bloody antlers, bows slung over their shoulders. A big powerful male might have eight points to his antlers. But is hard to tell how big my deer was since he is all shrunk up and missing parts now. Maybe he had eight points. Maybe six. I wish I knew. There are too many unknown factors. Sometimes I think I will never find them and I want to start crawling towards that dark space again. But the Almanac pulls me back. It helps me keep track of all the numbers. Every day a new mystery. It's all about looking closely enough, the way I looked closely at the dried insides of the deer until I found the heart. Everything has meaning. Like those ads that say "since 1962" and "since 1992." I have listed all those years and have uncovered the pattern: This is one of those years. Some-day they will say that Adam was here "since 2006" and then I will be part of the pattern too.

I hear a crow. Something is coming. I put the book inside my shirt to keep it safe and put my hand on the hatchet. Two people. Shouting "go away" does not work on people. It just brings them closer.

"Damion?" It is the skinny woman who's been here before, who yells. "Damion, are you there? I'm showing this property to this nice man and I want you to leave us alone, do you hear?"

Her voice gets low and lower like I can't hear, but I am able to detect even the slightest sound in the woods. It is what keeps me alive while death surrounds me.

"Weird kid from town," the skinny woman whispers to the "nice man." "Even though he's not really a kid anymore, except...here." The woman taps her head, where stubby girl antlers would be in another life. Her "nice man" nods, and looks around, a little afraid, while the skinny woman keeps talking and talking. "Ran away from the Home to live here in a hole. He's missing a few parts if you get my drift, but he's harmless. I'll call social services when we get back to the office, but you've got to admit, he's got taste. Look at that pretty little clearing. You build your cabin here, you can hunt without ever having to get up from the sofa. Now watch, he's probably crouching in that hole, but it's best to ignore him. I should have sent the state to clear him out long ago, but I'm just an old softie underneath."

They laugh and laugh, but nothing is funny. They don't know the truth even when it comes out their own mouths. Like the deer, we will all get soft underneath in time, food for the strange families of bugs in the universe. And that is a fact you can take to the bank.

For The Birds

PAYSON AND VALERIE Beckworth collapsed on the cobbled veranda with their gin and tonics. It had been a trying day, what with getting the new bird feeder positioned just so in the rose garden. Valerie's face hurt from having to smile through the ordeal of explaining to Lenny Akers from the service, not once, but twice (as if anyone had to be told at all!) about the gabled end of the feeder lining up visually with the gable of the house. Payson had to practically set the post himself—but that was all behind them now. The two Beckworths were thinking that it really had been worth all the bother.

"Isn't it just smashing?" asked Valerie.

Payson nodded and clinked his ice. "What about bird food?"

"Yes, yes," she said, batting at the air with her open hand, as if his question was something physical that could be pushed away. "It's coming. I sent away for a mix that attracts just the sort of birds we want."

Valerie leaned back in her cushioned chaise and pictured the garden maturing that year, exactly as that fey young man from the Landscape Studio had predicted. Right then and there she decided to let Suzanne Hollings know that, if asked, Valerie would not object to having the Shore Garden Club meet at her house in July.

The "Deluxe Songbird Mix" arrived late in June, and Valerie ratcheted the feeder down the pole herself, not trusting the job to Lenny. Soon enough, small, bright birds began to arrive, swooping and chirping, and being perfectly charming. At first, Valerie didn't even mind the mess of hulls under the feeder, but by the end of the week it was with genuine disgust that she discovered white splats on the shiny leaves of her heirloom roses.

Valerie had Lenny hand-wipe each soiled leaf with a damp cloth, but that was not nearly enough. She panicked as more birds arrived every day, and not the ones she had expected either, but hideous grackles and loud, piercing cowbirds.

"The little beggars will simply have to go elsewhere for a couple of weeks for their handouts," Valerie said to Payson at the end of a very long, very hot day. "We have to give the garden, and my nerves, time to recuperate before the Club date."

The bird seed was swiftly packed away, but the birds gave up hope reluctantly. Because of this, there were some Rosa 'Pompon Blanc Parfait' blooms that could not be saved from the digestive ends of the last of the feathered visitors, but Valerie bore it well and wrote it off to the caprice of Mother Nature.

When the thirty members of the Shore Garden Club arrived all went according to plan; Valerie could not have asked for more. The members lavished praise on the grounds and gardens, and especially the feeder. Everyone agreed that the faux sapling post really did seem to grow right up out of the dirt. They loved how the feeder's arches echoed the lines of house. It looked as if it had always been there. The club members said a great many things about it, but they were all too polite to mention—indeed, they were too polite to even notice—that the bird feeder had neither bird nor feed.

Valerie decided she would have these lovely women over again, soon.

Days after the last shrimp salad sandwich was thrown in the trash, and the punch bowl rinsed and put away, Valerie and Payson reminded each other that it was safe to put out the bird food again. Unfortunately, the bag of seed seemed to have been misplaced during the clean-up. The Beckworths both agreed that a new bag was needed, but soon it was one thing after another, and summers were short enough as they were.

Aquatic Ape

DUNCAN NOTED THE market price of lobsters. Cheap. Too cheap. Poor economic times had brought a halt to the purchase of luxuries like lobster, so the market was glutted with them. Cruise lines had cancelled millions of pounds of orders for the season and were serving cheap farmed shrimp from Asia instead of lobster in their surf and turf. While he waited for his takeout order at Manavilins Fish Shack, he picked up a copy of *New England Fisherman* to take his mind off his financial woes by reading about others' woes. Above the general noise of the restaurant, he heard a thickly accented voice rise from a booth.

"I am willing to make a contribution to nature, but nature must be willing to make a contribution to me first! Who is going to pay for me to change my nets?"

Duncan pressed his glasses hard against his face, as if that could block out the words. No matter which way he turned these days, his business problems lay in wait for him. This particular problem was

Kendrie Ottejnstein, captain of a hundred-ton South African vessel fishing out of Port Ellery for the herring season, and there he sat, trapped by Annuncia, whose physique was as solid as if she'd been poured in a foundry. Kendrie was a fish she'd been trying to land for a long time, and all she had to do to block his exit from his booth was pull up a chair. Aside from her job managing Seacrest's, she was an organizer for Green Fish, a group that promoted ecologically caught seafood. She was constantly haranguing captains like Kendrie—a paying Seacrest's client—about conforming to practices that respected the fisheries, such as proper net size to limit bycatch, the inadvertent capture of one species while trying to fish for another. By law, the bycatch—which was almost always dead, and, if not dead, dying—had to be thrown back into the sea. It couldn't even be given to Duncan to dehydrate at Seacrest's, which was a truly sinful waste of an already depleted resource. Duncan understood the long-term consequences of dirty fishing, but with Seacrest's on such shaky legs at the moment, this was hardly the time to alienate clients because of it.

"It's cheaper to pay the fines than to change my nets," continued Kendrie. "You know how much that costs?"

"Do you know how much it costs not to?" asked Annuncia. She spoke with controlled motions of her hand. "Healthy fisheries are good business, good for everyone. If the fish disappear, so do we."

"I'll be here," he said, his mouth full of coleslaw.

"No, Kendrie, not you." With this she tapped him on the forehead, and he gave her a serious look of warning. She pushed her chair back with a purposefully grating sound. "You may be clever, Kendrie, but you're not very smart."

Duncan hid behind a pillar so Kendrie wouldn't see him and cancel their contract on the spot. The week before, the captain of a factory trawler left Seacrest's for a waste processor in Portland to get away from Annuncia's public attacks. She accused him of scraping the bottom of the ocean floor clean with his trawl, the marine equivalent of clear-cutting rain forest.

"Duncan!" Slocum called from the kitchen. "Put a piece of lemon in your mouth!"

Duncan picked up a wedge from a bowl and stared at it. Manavilins was owned by his buddy Slocum Statler, whose bread and butter was the fry plates, but he dreamed of making a name for himself in gastro-aquatic wonders, as he called them, and flew a pirate's flag in the kitchen. The calamari calzone wasn't half bad, if you could get past the disturbing menu notes: *Squid are generally recognized to be smarter than dogs. Endangered status: Zero. Because of warming waters, squid have surpassed humans in total biomass on the planet.*

"It's a test," Slocum said, wiping his hands on his apron as he approached the takeout counter from the kitchen. He had an ancient mariner gleam in his eyes and a full, squared-off beard and walrus mustache, probably in violation of the health code. It made him look like an Old Testament prophet, which made people trust him more than they should. He was wider than Duncan but just as tall, and it was this height that had bound them together in elementary school. They saw life from the same perspective, above the fray and into the future, full of hope. Slocum had kept his dreams, no matter how daft, while Duncan had slipped blindly into the family business. He couldn't even remember what it was he once wanted to do with his life.

"A test of what?" asked Duncan.

"Lemon juice makes introverts salivate more than extroverts. This is for Clover's kid's science project. Open." He squeezed the lemon on Duncan's tongue. "Now don't swallow for a minute."

Clover was Slocum's sometimes girlfriend, who wore tight pleather jeans low on her hips, with a huge belt buckle centered on her pelvis. They'd met when she rode through town with her motorcycle gang years ago and have continued happily in this way for years, her coming and going whenever. Right now, she was in New Mexico while her preteen son, Harley, was staying with Slocum above the restaurant. She often left Harley in Port Ellery for months while she was on the road, to give him some stability.

"Time to get with the program, Kendrie," Annuncia said to the red-faced South African. "You might call yourself a captain, but you don't know dick about fishing." With that, she stood up slowly and walked away.

"Time's up," said Slocum, brandishing a flashlight. "Tip your noggin and let's get a look." Duncan opened his mouth for inspection, and while his head was bent back, he read the hand-lettered sign tacked over the counter: *No trans fats used in cooking.* What the sign didn't say was that Manavilins used lard for frying, and Slocum often claimed he'd use whale blubber if he could get his hands on any. He believed that fat was the secret to the success of the species. Humans were not just the fattest primates, they also had ten times as many fat cells as would be expected in any animal of its size, which, to Slocum, pointed to one obvious conclusion: Humans were descended from aquatic apes. And, he believed, they needed to maintain those fat deposits for when—perhaps not so far in the future—the rising tides of global warming forced Homo sapiens back to the sea.

"Hmm," Slocum said at last. "No response." He gave Duncan a worried look, then smiled. "We'll have to preserve you in a specimen jar and bring you to the science fair—the non-responsive wonder."

Annuncia appeared at Duncan's side. She was still in her work clothes. Her red smock, with SEACREST's embroidered in white on the pocket, strained at the hips and was streaked with black fish powder. Her bushel of dark hair was pulled up under a tight red snood. "Hull-sucking sea worm," she said, turning back to face Kendrie, who did not look up from his mountain of onion rings. "There are fishermen who make a living fishing, and then there's an industry that wants to make a killing," she said even louder. When Kendrie refused to rise to the bait, she picked up her takeout bag. "Don't look at me like that, Dun'n."

"We need every customer we can get right now, Annuncia. Don't single him out for killing off the human race. You're as subtle as a pile driver."

"Whale balls. Puddingheads like Kendrie, they've got to understand what the stakes are. It's not like we can go somewhere else when we fuck it all up. *This* band of temperature, *this* mix of oxygen—it's all we can live in, and it all depends on the ocean to keep it stable. Kendrie's Neanderthal skull can't compute that saving the ocean means saving his own sorry ass."

"Can this wait until *our* business is a little more stable?" Duncan whispered.

"Dun'n, don't compromise yourself for money."

"I have nothing left to compromise myself for."

She looked around the restaurant. "Where's Wade? He's giving me a ride home."

"Here!" Wade, Seacrest's head of maintenance, stepped out of the walk-in cooler behind Slocum. After work, he sometimes ran fish from his cousin's boat to local restaurants. He wanted to save family fishing boats in the same way that family farms had become a national cause. He was so disgusted with the corporately owned industrial fleet that he frowned on Seacrest's accepting its fish waste, which was substantial. Between Wade's local fishing and Annuncia's green fish, Duncan felt as if the financial health of Seacrest's was far down on his employees' lists of priorities.

"We're leaving, Dun'n," said Annuncia. "Come on, Wade. See you Monday, boss."

"Wait." Wade picked up a *Support local fishing* bumper sticker from a pile on the counter and handed one to Duncan. "I know you'll want one of these. To save the fishes." And with this he slapped his heart.

"Of course," said Duncan, and he moved to put it in his pocket, but Wade pulled it from his grasp.

"I'll put it on the truck for you on my way out," he said. "No problem."

Duncan cringed. Yes, local boats needed every extra consideration to survive, but so did he. He hoped Kendrie, or any of the other factory boat captains, would not recognize his truck.

When the door closed behind them, he looked around the restaurant, as long and narrow as a shipping container, filled with the comforting warmth of human bodies. Young lovers dipped fried oysters in tartar sauce and brought them to each other's mouths; children licked ketchup from white paper cups and got it on their noses; married couples eyed dishes sprung from Slocum's misplaced imagination, smiled, and dared each other to go first. They were happy. Duncan could be happy. He should let Seacrest's sink or swim on its own. He could not play God; he could not part the sea. And besides, maybe next week business would pick up. He felt light and free at the thought, as if he were floating above his earthly troubles. He smiled as he saw Slocum pack up his order, he smiled as he handed him the credit card, and he kept right on smiling past the point when his card was rejected.

"Sorry," said Slocum, handing it back to him. "I'm supposed to cut it in half," he whispered. "But you keep it. Pay me whenever. And wait." He held up a batter-coated finger and called to a waitress. "Bag up a special for Duncan here."

Duncan adjusted his glasses as if it had all been a matter of faulty vision. Either an embarrassing silence had swept across the room or he had a case of hysterical deafness. Slocum placed a bag on top of his box. "Pulpo gallego! That'll cure what ails you." He put a hand on Duncan's shoulder. "Call me, my friend, we'll get you back on course. Remember—a dead calm comes before a new wind."

Duncan gave him a sickly smile and left. In a time like this, if all his best friend could do was to give him some oily octopus and a maritime platitude for comfort, then the end could not be very far away.

Live Magical Moments

Live Magical Moments in this custom built contemp
on beautifully landscaped grounds, trellised arbors, gardens
with an air of time-warp containment. Water garden and
orchard all add up to a dream come true.

Feeling like an impostor in jeans and gardening clogs, Andrea
MacPherson sat on the teak bench and gazed out at the quiet street
beyond her redwood fence. She ignored the flower beds in her line of
vision as best she could, but the aggressive colors seemed to scream
for her attention. A radioactive-pink mound of azalea positively
glowed. She adjusted her sunglasses, which both protected and hid
her eyes, then let her freckled hand rest back down on the manila
folder in her lap, a gesture which made her think of other folders,
other waiting. With both hands, she picked up the folder and put
her cheek to it, feeling the coolness of the stiff paper against her
skin and closed her eyes as if she might just drift off. She wanted

to drift off—far off. Then she snorted at herself for being such an idiot. This folder might feel like a fat medical chart but it was only garden instructions. Only. Thirty typed pages with bonus charts, lists, photographs, and telephone numbers. Too bad a bank account didn't come with it as well. The company that the Durells had used was far too expensive, and if the truth be told—and why not tell the truth?—Andrea felt inferior to both the service and the gardens. Worse, she felt invisible. A nursery truck heavy with every conceivable piece of motorized equipment just showed up one day in March without her calling, releasing a team of mowers and blowers upon her yard as if there hadn't been a change of owners at all, as if she were just an interchangeable cash machine in the life of the gardens. The first bill was as much as her mortgage payment, and after two visits in which there was a lot of pitiful head-shaking on the part of the workers, she said enough.

A tree limb hung over the bench like an arm and a small khaki-colored bird landed on it, swearing voraciously in her direction. A wren, maybe, but what type of tree? Andrea had intended to build up a gardening library over the winter but she'd only gotten as far as the remainders bin at Walgreens where she picked up a book called Managing the Plant. It was about assembly line mechanics and that was the last time she even made an effort. The wren made a show of swooping to within a foot of Andrea's head, then raced back up to the branch again, which made Andrea think her presence posed a threat to some hidden nest. She sat very still and tried to keep her leg from its restless swinging. The bird turned its head and eyed her with suspicion, then gave up, flapping off on its busy day. Well, Andrea was very busy today too. After months of neglect and inept meddling on her part, something had to be done with the property before it deteriorated altogether, so she tried a number she found posted on the bulletin board at the supermarket: Garden Chores: Call Jim. She liked that he called it for what it was, a chore, and didn't try to dress it up with "landscape" this and "designer" that. He was on his way right now to have a look, but she wasn't getting her hopes up. No more expectations. It was hard to imagine now how eager she'd once been, ready to lose herself in the mysteries of nature. She thought she'd be speaking horticultural Latin with kindred souls by the end of the year, but she soon discovered that a garden relied almost entirely on human intervention and had precious little to do with nature. She didn't know that yet, though, when last October, right before they closed on the house, Mrs. Durell asked Andrea to meet her in the gardens for a walk and talk. Andrea had come from a bank appointment in a wool suit and heels, which was her first mistake. Her second was in not running for the hills.

Mrs. Durell, dressed in coordinated slacks and sweater of vegetable shades of green, had met her at the front gate, a pseudo-Japanese affair constructed of dark timbers and some kind of clinging vine. The entrance was thickly cosseted on either side with flower beds, except that there were no flowers, it being late October. All the leaves were spotted and tired, even to Andrea's untrained eyes. Visually, there was nothing to admire, but there was an interesting fragrance in the air. Andrea sniffed in deeply. "Mmm. What's that lovely smell?"

Mrs. Durell raised her well-shaped nose and closed her eyes. She was a short woman, much older than Andrea, but deeply tanned and well maintained, oddly wide in the shoulders, with a no-nonsense bob of gray hair. Andrea felt absolutely wanton with her auburn curls and modest décolletage peaking out from her tailored jacket. "Mulch," Mrs. Durell said definitively, then talked at length about the competing charms of shredded redwood and cocoa shells.

"But enough of that," she said cheerfully. "I'm sure you'll choose the mulch that's best for you and your family."

Family? As Mrs. Durell led the way through the yard, clutching the folder firmly under her arm, Andrea felt herself sinking deeper into the gravel path with every step. Never mind family, she barely had a husband. Eric was an army surgeon, and he'd had to go back to his old post in Germany for a few weeks while she set up their new civilian life here, near the teaching hospital and the small scrap of family she could claim as her own blood. Mica, her brother's widow, had moved to town with a new husband and her two girls from her marriage with Warren. Andrea felt a twitch of resentment that in mid-life Warren had been able to have a second batch of kids, whereas she could not even have a first. Then she felt a flood of guilt—it was wrong to think evil thoughts of the deceased. At any rate, Andrea had decided that if she couldn't be a mother then she would be an aunt, but Warren's son was distant in both miles and emotion, and Mica and the girls had such regimented lives they were often too busy for her. When Eric returned he would be very busy too. But even if he had nothing to do, he was not concerned about domestic matters and would have no mulch preferences. It would all fall on her. As always. With all this clutter in her head, she had trouble concentrating on Mrs. Durell's impromptu seminar on path maintenance: what stone to refresh them with every year, where to order it, where to have it dumped so it didn't get in the grass, and what to do about any weeds that dared to spring up between the gravel. Mrs. Durell seemed to have a religious devotion to Round-Up.

"I won't be using any chemicals," said Andrea, stirring from her grim reverie. "I'm going to garden naturally."

Mrs. Durell took no offense and laughed, even waving a hand to indicate 'get out of here.' "Everyone says that in the beginning," she said. "But that conviction doesn't stick. To do it right, you have to bring out the big guns. Besides, I can't imagine Terry putting up with that for very long."

Terry was the owner of the service that Andrea could not

afford, but of course, back then, she had no conception of what it took to take on a project of this size. The woodland path had as many twists and turns as a bowel, laid out not as an efficient means to get from one place to another, but to display the Durell's collection of shrubs, which, back in the fall, had varied only in shades of deteriorating foliage. Everything was carefully spaced—not one tree, shrub, or plant touched one another. "It really is magical when it's all in bloom and the sunlight filters through the trees," sighed Mrs. Durell, to which all Andrea could add was a wistful "oh." At the end of this convoluted path, the vista opened up and they came upon a half dozen gnarly old trees. "We think of each part of the property as a room of its own," Mrs. Durell explained. "This is the orchard room." She bent down and petted the grass, as luscious and napped as a baby seal. "You can't see a trace of them now, of course, but narcissus are naturalized all through these trees in large swaths."

"So...narcissus," said Andrea tentatively, "are they like daffodils?"

Mrs. Durell either didn't hear the question or purposely ignored it. "It's mostly "Pheasant's Eye" but some early blooming "King Alfred" as well. They're so carefree. A little bone meal in the spring, and every few years divide after flowering but before dying back." She stood up and smiled at the unseen bulbs in the ground. "The best thing about them is that the deer hate them."

"Deer come into the yard?" Andrea looked around her as

if she might see Bambi come bouncing out of the verge. "That would be fun."

Mrs. Durell went pale and put her hand on Andrea's wrist. "You don't mean that," she said. "Believe me, the first time you come out to find that your tulips have been eaten to the quick... All your work, your dreams and careful planning, gone overnight." She put on a brave smile and slapped her folder. "I've made a chart of where all the narcissus are, and when you might expect them. My favorite catalogue is Van Engels. Order before July to get the best selection."

"They're annuals?" It was one of the few gardening words Andrea knew at the time, gleaned from the real estate agent's sales pitch during her first walkthrough. "The gardens are largely perennial," Leslie had explained. "You don't have to replant every year like you do with annuals. Just sit back and enjoy!" Andrea realized now that Leslie probably never had a garden in her life.

"Annuals?" Mrs. Durell looked straight at Andrea and gave a little worried laugh. "I don't play games with hardiness. These are the good old-fashioned workhorses of spring. You order more every year because you want to order more every year."

"So, you don't have to replant them from seed?"

Mrs. Durell froze for moment then took in a breath, as if summoning some terrible strength. "Andrea, you don't replant these from seed at all. You plant bulbs to replace winterkill."

"Winter kill?" When Andrea had signed the purchase and sale

agreement, her garden fantasies, such as they were, were firmly set in the spring. She'd never considered that she'd have to first get past winter and its accompanying barrenness.

"Oh," Mrs. Durell said, as if she'd been stung by a bee. "You know not to mow the grass under the trees until the narcissus leaves start turning brown?"

Andrea nodded slowly. "The trees. What are those again?" She'd only been up to this area once, during the showing, and she hadn't been all that focused. She'd seen it all in a daze, like a passing dream.

"Apples," Mrs. Durell said flatly, and Andrea realized that a couple of the trees were covered with bright red fruit. She said "ah" knowing she sounded like a complete idiot.

"We don't want the late bearers to be a burden for you," Mrs. Durell continued. "We'll harvest before we leave unless you'd rather we didn't. That one over there is 'Keepsake' and should be just about perfect now."

Andrea's heels dug into the smooth pelt of lawn as she walked closer to the tree, and she felt Mrs. Durell's eyes on the marks she left behind. She reached up for an apple and took a tentative bite, which instantly transported her to an abandoned orchard of her childhood. It was probably a housing development now, but back then she had climbed the trees and fought apple wars with Warren from the safety of the branches. She was about to take another bite when she remembered Mrs. Durell's love of chemicals. "They're lovely," said Andrea. "But you take them. I'll have my own next year."

"Only if you're diligent," warned Mrs. Durell, closely inspecting an apple without removing it from the tree. She seemed pleased at what she found, or didn't find, and turned her attention to Andrea. "Remember to rake the windfall as soon as it lands and the same with the leaves, otherwise they create a breeding ground for blight. Watch for borers, spray against loopers. Make sure you wait until winter to prune. If you do it too early, you'll stimulate new growth that will be vulnerable later on. Most of all, don't let your guard down when it comes to deer—keep the fence hot even when you think you're safe." She paused, looking around. "What I've forgotten, Terry will remember. We've been a great team, and I know you will too." She gave Andrea a tender smile as if she were marrying them off, then she turned and walked away.

As soon as Mrs. Durell disappeared down a path, Andrea pitched the uneaten apple over the high fence with its mean little electric wire running along the top. Maybe a deer stood on the other side, waiting and praying for an apple to fall its way. She hurried to catch up with Mrs. Durell. "What else needs pruning?"

"Cut back spring bloomers in summer, summer bloomers in the spring," she said, and then abruptly stopped at a long double row of tired foliage. "This is the 'peony room' and this particular beauty is 'Carnivale.' My mother gave me the original rhizome from her own garden. It doesn't look like much now, but when it's in bloom..."

There was a pause as Mrs. Durell collected her emotions. Andrea understood that this was a difficult move for her. The Durells had built the house themselves, a basic fifties modern suburban, raised five children here, and planted every blade of grass together, side by side. "There was nothing here when they started," Leslie had enthused, and Andrea had been sold on the miracle of creation. Now the Durells were moving to the Southwest for Mr. Durell's health. It must have been a hard decision for them, having to choose between the garden and his life.

With a shake of her head, Mrs. Durell was off and running again. "Peonies want to drag in the mud so stake them before they go down, it's too late to do anything about it afterwards. We've pulled the bamboo stakes and left them in the garden shed for you, and there's plenty of jute too, in the right-hand drawer of the potting table."

Mrs. Durell smiled at Andrea so Andrea smiled back. She had no idea what this woman was talking about. "Thank you, yes, that will be very helpful." Then Mrs. Durell led the way to another "room."

Andrea should have bolted right then, sacrificing the deposit in exchange for a guilt-free life. She never pruned the apple trees that winter. She hadn't sprayed either, since she'd never gotten around to researching organic alternatives to Mrs. Durell's poisons. Maybe that was why the apple leaves were black and the pea-sized fruit stunted and falling to the ground. It was too late for them, but maybe this Jim guy could save the rest. The garden needed so much from her and she had nothing to give. According to Leslie, the Durells were so pleased to have the MacPhersons take on the gardens because they were young—although at forty-one, Andrea felt absolutely ancient—and seemed "up to the task." Andrea had been so excited that the words had flown right over her head. She had thought that a garden was a finite object to be bought and sold, but now she knew, a garden cannot be purchased ready-made. From the bench, she turned so she could see the peonies, already in bud, or "au point" as Mrs. Durell would have called their delicate condition. As she had predicted, they were dragging their heavy heads in the mud and would soon bloom in the dirt. Andrea had never even looked for the bamboo and jute. She absently picked at a loose thread on her jeans. Peonies and apples weren't her only failures. The mums and asters in the back yard that were so vibrant in the fall—"the last blast" as Mrs. Durell called them—now looked like a patch of weeds. "Pinch them three times before the Fourth of July," she'd said, but what did that mean? This might be nature, but it wasn't very natural. There was so much manipulation. And she hated this timing stuff. She just wouldn't do it.

She began swinging her leg again in agitation, the nest be damned. She'd gotten herself into this mess, now she had to find a way out. The property was not much more than an acre but it was too much for her. Aside from the paths and apple trees, there were hundreds of feet of borders to tend to, a rock garden, a rose arbor and a fountain. The place had everything but a labyrinth. Andrea had thought she wanted to have her hands full, but what did she know? She'd grown up in an apartment in the city, with a small edge of brown grass between the sidewalk and the building. Her early married life was spent on an army base in Germany, and when they came back to the states, they had lived in motels until Eric figured out where they were going to settle. All those years she had her pregnancy project to keep her busy, which she only gave up last summer with the fourth miscarriage. They talked about adopting, but her heart wasn't in it. She still cried spontaneously during the day. Then Warren's sudden and bizarre death in the middle of it all almost crushed her. More loss, more mortality in her face. When this house came up for sale with its beautiful gardens, she thought it was a gift to soothe her sorrow. Now all this growth and fecundity only served to increase it.

"Remember." Mrs. Durell had said through her tears as she was saying goodbye. "We communicate to the plants by understanding their needs, and they communicate to us by thriving. Or not."

On that dismal note, the Durells moved out and the MacPhersons moved in. Andrea hadn't even finished unpacking when the first frost came and stripped the gardens of their leaves, making the land stark and exposed overnight. Soon snow covered the earth and the bare winter forms became still lifes. One day in January, not able to stand another moment in the house, Andrea had wandered up an icy path and discovered a sundial in the rock garden. She brushed the snow off the dial's raised bronze lettering hoping for some uplifting, summery message only to find *Be About Your Business, For Night Cometh*. What sort of thing was that to have in a garden? She never really shook the feeling of dread she felt that day, and in the spring, instead of looking forward to the slow miracle of nature unfolding she felt flattened by it, even afraid. She'd failed at the garden and it had failed her.

She was just thinking she should stand up, maybe even pick up a hose so she'd look like she knew what she was about, when a beat-up Toyota truck pulled up to the curb. She was relieved that there was no trailer loaded with industrial gardening machines behind it. A tall man with a braid down his back got out of the driver's side and raised his hand. It had been a long time she'd seen a braid on a man—it was not a common hairstyle on military bases, not even on women. Under high, burnt cheekbones, he had a short beard speckled with gray. He was older than she was, and she hoped wiser. He looked a little like Willie Nelson and there was nothing wrong with that. He moved towards the gate and she felt herself slip into a funk. She was so tired of having to talk about the garden. She wondered if she should just cut her losses and get out. Buy a condo or a planned community where maintenance was taken care of by someone else.

"Hello there." He called in a pleasant raspy voice. "Mrs. MacPherson?"

She smiled and waved him on in. He opened the pseudo-Japanese gate with difficulty. The mystery vine had been growing with such vigor it seemed about to seal her in, like in a fairy tale. She tried not to take it personally, since there was no point in being angry at nature. He ripped a length of vine out of his way and tossed it into the bushes. Her kind of guy. He wore canvas pants and a maroon t-shirt with an open and untucked denim shirt over that, and the best part was, he did not carry a clipboard. There'd be no inscrutable note-taking and head-shaking today. As he moved through the front yard, he seemed very amused by something and made no special effort to stay on the path as he surveyed the intricate layout of curvy beds and borders. The azalea seemed to jump out and startle him. It had certainly shocked her when it first opened the week before. It was so pink it didn't even seem alive, but it was probably the one thing she couldn't kill if she tried.

"Jim Pelligrino," he said. He approached the bench with a slight bend to his back and squinted his eyes so tightly she couldn't tell what color they were. He held his hand out to her. It was wide and thickly calloused, with deeply ingrained lines of dirt like a Dutch engraving. Andrea extended her rather virginal hand to him, almost letting the folder slip from her lap.

"Andrea," she said. "The place is a mess," she blurted out with a nervous laugh. She always fell apart around professionals, even professionals in Birkenstock sandals. She did not make a very good doctor's wife because of it. She made a worse patient.

"Nonsense," he said, looking around him with a nod. "A garden that looks relaxed puts a soul right at ease."

She patted the bench. "Have a seat."

"Let me guess," he said, taking the folder from her lap when he was settled. "The instructions that came with the gardens." He opened it up and paged through the loose sheets of paper. "'Mow and rake the lawn in one direction only?' Good God."

"The previous owner said it would get a fungus if I didn't," said Andrea.

"There's six pages here just on the watering system." He looked up and studied a patch of grass in front of them. The lawn was no longer a fine green pelt, but a dry global mix of broadleaf weeds. "How's that working out for you?"

"It's not," Andrea admitted. "The emitters must be clogged or something." She wanted to tell him it wasn't her fault. The Durells had made it all so complicated with miles of tubes that had to be flushed and monitored and repaired. It was just easier to take out a hand-held hose and hope for the best.

Jim nodded and placed the papers on the ground. "So those are their plans," he said. "Any of your own?"

Andrea frowned and stared at the unkempt borders. "Yes. I plan to buy a lottery ticket."

Jim gave a little laugh. "It's a showcase, all right," he said. "But it's their dream, not yours."

Andrea looked around and shrugged. "I felt like I was adopting her baby instead of buying her garden." The words caught in her throat and her heart beat faster. She was ashamed to still be having such a reaction every time the word "baby" was uttered, but she couldn't help it. She was emotionally dehydrated from her fertility ordeal, and tears were all she had left. Jim, gratefully, was not looking at her. He was gazing around at the garden and seemed lost in his own thoughts.

"Well," he said at last. "Even so, you have options."

"What sort?" she said, with not much hope. The sculpted landscape looked so firmly rooted in place it seemed incapable of change.

"You can tear it down or you can work with what you have. Or anything in between. Do you even like it?"

She raised her hands and let them fall back to her lap. "It's not that I don't like it, I just don't know what I'm doing, and I can't afford too much expertise. I had no idea there was this sort of work involved. And I had no idea there would be this." She pointed to the pink gash of azalea and Jim grimaced, which made her smile.

"It's pretty simple. If you can't or won't take all this on, you've got to decide what you want and let go of the rest."

"But I don't know what I want," Andrea said in almost a whisper.

"You will. Concentrate your effort on one thing. A little success'll give you some confidence."

It was embarrassing to admit that there wasn't any part of her own property that didn't intimidate her. She pointed to some shrubby stumps. "I tried to prune, but even with all this guidance," and she pointed to the open folder on the ground, "I didn't know what I was doing. I just started with the clompers, and the next thing I knew..."

Jim stood up. She saw now that he had a slight limp, but he knelt on one knee without much difficulty and fondled a few brave leaves emerging from the battered branches. "A beauty bush. This year's buds are gone, but next year it's going to be super. You have to bring these monsters right to the ground every once in a while and start again. You've got good instincts."

Andrea was surprised, and pleased. She stood up and stepped over the folder. "Come here," she said, and they walked around the house so she could show him a raggedy patch of plants. "I'm worried that the mums and asters won't bloom. I didn't pinch."

"They'll be lovely no matter what you do or don't do. They won't be tight little cushions, like at the nurseries, but they'll be taller, more natural. The butterflies prefer them that way."

"Butterflies. That would be nice." She thought ahead to the fall. She imagined herself at the end of the season, basking in some sort of accomplishment, even if it was only a single butterfly. It had been a long time since she thought about the future. "What about dead-heading? Mrs. Durell used that word a lot. I haven't done anything for fear of making a mistake."

"Let me tell you about deadheading." With an expert flick of his fingers, Jim nipped a faded bloom from a daisy. "If you don't do it, there will be more energy put into seed-making than the root. The seeds will fall off, provide food for birds, and those that make it through the winter will make new plants, if you give it half a chance and don't drench the ground with weedkiller. On the other hand, if you keep cutting off the spent blooms, you'll get more blooms because it keeps plants in a state of frustrated motherhood."

"It sounds so...invasive."

Jim shrugged and let the bloom fall from his fingers. "There's nothing innocent about a garden. You've got to be willing to get a little blood on your hands."

They meandered around to the back yard, and Andrea looked at her freckly hands. Never mind blood, she didn't even have any dirt on them. Not so much as a chipped nail. It looked as though she hadn't tried at all. An arch led out to the trash area, heavily camouflaged with lattice and climbing roses, which only brought attention to the very thing it was meant to hide. "I call this the garbage room," said Andrea, and they both laughed. He was on her side. There was no reason to linger where they were, so they headed up to the orchard. She didn't say anything as they walked the path but Jim nodded as if listening to some master gardener in his head. He bent down and pointed to the remnants of a plant.

"Hosta," he said. "Or was, until deer ate it. Is that fence on?"

She shook her head. "I don't want to hurt them, and besides, I've never even seen one."

"They're here. Jumping in for a quick bite now and again."

They continued walking, and when it opened up to the orchard, Andrea regretted that the daffodils—or narcissus, as Mrs. Durell called them—were done. It had been a beautiful, bucolic show. The trees had been in bloom at the same time, covered with small pinky-white flowers whose petals fell like snowflakes on the daffodils which seemed to ache with openness. The Durells had gotten it right, but it happened way up here where Andrea couldn't enjoy it. She had come upon it by accident.

"Any prayer for the apples?" she asked.

"Too late for this year," Jim said, scratching his thumbnail on a smutty leaf. "You might get a few in the fall if you're willing to put up with imperfections. If you want more than that, we'll talk over the winter about an organic spraying schedule. And if you're not going to use the electric fencing, we'll have to mix some pepper spray for the deer. They've already eaten all the young tips they could reach."

Andrea fondled the shredded end of a branch and smiled, thinking of the tender mouth that had pulled on it. Then they headed back to the house.

"Is that a fountain?" Jim looked down a side path which led to the 'water room.' "There's high maintenance for you."

"The fish died," said Andrea. "When the ice melted this spring they floated to the surface."

"Poor things," Jim said.

Andrea answered with a painful nod and then she felt tears gathering. She hadn't shed a single tear for the fish, but now she saw she'd caused their death with her own ignorance. She might have saved them if she'd only looked for the instructions and done everything she was told. Or not. Maybe they would have died no matter what she did. For all she knew, Mrs. Durell ordered a new batch every spring, along with the bulbs, to make up for winterkill. Warren had died a watery death too. He'd gone head-to-head with nature and lost, but at least he'd left behind his children. What would she leave? She stared at the lifeless water garden, where the stone cherub should be perpetually peeing into the basin of green slime. She didn't even know how to turn on the water.

"Look," said Jim. He pointed to the front yard but made no move towards it. "There they go."

She turned to see the papers blowing across the yard, scattering them to all corners of the property like graceful white birds. Some blew over the fence, dancing down the street, a few got caught in an upward spiral and landed back on her spectacularly imperfect lawn.

A couple of sheets tumbled into the thicket of trees, where a ray of sunlight made the paper brilliant against the dark. She and Jim continued to stand there, just staring, as if it was happening to someone else, somewhere else. She sniffed and realized she was crying.

"I'm so sorry," she said, taking off her sunglasses to wipe her face with the back of her hand. "I don't know what keeps coming over me."

"Here's a plan," he said. "We go easy on ourselves this year, keep track of what you like and don't like. A little nudge here, a little there, we enhance nature instead of controlling it, and in a few years it'll be all yours."

"Years?" Andrea snorted. "I'll be an old woman."

"Nonsense. You'll just be getting started. A garden is born again every spring. It'll keep you young."

She wanted to believe in the healing power of nature. She wanted to believe, period, and was about to say something to that effect when Jim pointed through the trees and whispered "Shh." Andrea took in a sharp breath when she saw the deer, so neatly camouflaged against the foliage. It must have been nearby the whole time, but Jim had only seen it because it had been spooked by the paper and moved. Now it was still again, ears up and alert, deep watery eyes staring at them. Only rapidly dilating nostrils gave it away as a living, breathing creature. It did not even move when a fawn moved slowly up behind it, all soft and spotted, clinging to the shadows.

When You Are Done Being Happy

WHEN YOU ARE done being happy, kneel in front of the cabinet at the far end of the kitchen. It is the place you stored all the things you thought you might need someday, but won't. Look behind the tortilla press you bought twenty years ago, right before fresh tortillas became widely available in the supermarkets, making it obsolete. Find the kit for baking a checkerboard birthday cake. It remains unopened, even though you often thought of it, but there was never enough time for a project of that magnitude. There was only the rush for a store-bought cake, or in a good year, homemade cupcakes with canned frosting. If the children cared, they kept that information to themselves. They are gone, but the checkerboard cake pans are still waiting for you. Take them out now. You have the time.

When you are done being happy, think back to a list you made when you were fifteen years old and so miserable you wanted to fly out of your body. When you made a poorly thought-out attempt in that direction you broke both ankles. The hospital psychiatrist told you to write a list of all the good things that lay ahead of you, to think of the future instead of relentlessly probing your immediate sores.

"Like what?" you asked.

"Falling in love," the doctor said with some impatience in his voice. "Marriage, children."

"You're shitting me, right?"

"No. Those are generally the things that make women happy."

The next day you brought him a list. You'd pressed down so hard on the pencil it could be read with a finger.

I will not fall in love.

I will not marry.

I will not have children.

The doctor glanced at the paper and put it down on his desk. He looked out the window and neither of you spoke for the rest of the session.

When you are done being happy, go to the supermarket. Push the cart past the groceries you bought there over the years. The Special K, the Jones sausage, the breaded chicken cutlets. The things your husband once ate. The things he loved. Travel the aisles like a tourist. Admire the mountains of canned goods, adjust a box of fusilli on the bottom shelf. Feel the cool air of the freezer bins on your face. Smile at the other shoppers. Buy nothing. Want nothing. Leave the empty cart in the parking lot at such an angle that the slightest breeze will send it rolling into that black Escalade hogging up three spaces.

When you are done being happy, take up origami. Start with the pile of paper on your desk, the unread correspondence that grows wild and rank with each passing week. Pick a card, any card, fold it in half, then a quarter. Repeat until you have a tight little condolence cube and the only word showing is Loss.

"Why did you try to hurt yourself?" the doctor had asked some weeks after the list incident. You were at the Home by then. You were never told if your parents were unwilling to take you back, or not allowed. It was a relief either way.

"I have nothing to say about that," you said.

"We need to make a plan of action," he said. "Things you can do if those thoughts come back."

"What thoughts?" you asked.

He looked at his hands. In the same way that oncologists never say the word cancer to the cancerous, psychiatrists never say the word suicide to the suicidal.

"You understand," he said. "There is no self-destruction without the destruction of others."

"I understand completely," you said. "The Celts used to remove the brains of their dead kings and mix them with lime to make brain balls. They were their most powerful weapons."

He had nothing to say about that.

When you are done being happy, decide that life is not a list of events to be experienced but a set of questions to be answered, and not the sort of question you used to ask, like, is the eye really the only bloodless organ? You must ask yourself the big questions. Why are you here? What is the purpose of life? Do this while you bake the checkerboard cake. Halfway into the recipe, realize you neglected to buy the ingredients you needed at the supermarket. Instead of contemplating the meaning of life, you must now ask the universe if baking soda will work just as well as baking powder. There is no answer, and that is your answer. Just keep moving.

When you are done being happy, and the three sunken layers of the checkerboard cake are cooling on metal racks, pull out the box of stationary from the bottom drawer of your desk. Break the seal. This is the marbled paper your son brought back from Florence his junior year abroad, right before everyone started to use email and stopped writing letters. Make a new list on this obsolete sheet.

There is no hope of joy except in human relations.

There is no hope of joy except in human relations.

There is no hope of joy except in human relations.

When you are done being happy, go feed the cake to the ducks at the pond. Toss the crumbs by the handful onto the surface of the water and watch the birds fly towards you from all directions. Pay attention to how they land heels first, spraying water into the air ahead of them. Notice how they keep their wings wide open to break their fall. Throw with wild abandon, so that everyone gets a little.

Acknowledgments

Reef of Plagues

"Reef of Plagues" was commissioned as a part of "Reading the Currents. Stories from the 21st Century Sea," a project by the International Literature Festival Berlin 2017 in cooperation with the Science Year 2016*17 Seas and Oceans (an initiative by the Federal Ministry of Education and Research, Germany).

The Hopper, March 2019

Fire & Water, Stories from the Anthropocene anthology, Black Lawrence Press, August 2021

Highwire Act

3 Elements, Issue 28, Fall 2020

Dreams for a Broken World anthology, Essential Dreams Press, November 2022

It Won't Be Long Now *Winds of Change: Short Stories About Our Climate*, Dragonfly Publications, 2015

Among Animals 2 anthology, Ashland Creek Press, 2016

Infant Kettery Excerpted from the novel *Arroyo Circle*, forthcoming from Green Writers Press, October 2024

Flying Home Stonecoast Review, June 2021

Among Animals 3 anthology, Ashland Creek Press, 2022

Excerpted from the novel *Arroyo Circle*, forthcoming from Green Writers Press, October 2024

Good Job, Robin Slate.com, Future Tense, February 2022

Transform the World anthology, OWI, Fall 2023

Float Bear Deluxe Magazine, #31, Winter 2010-2011

Winner of the Doug Fir Fiction Award, Orlo.org, Excerpted from the novel *Float*, which was still in progress, published in 2013 by Ashland Creek Press

Thirteen Minutes   Santa Ana River Review, Spring 2018,
                          Vol 3, Issue 2

Organic, Local, and   daCunha, February 2019
Cruelty-Free

Huldufólk   Prime Number Magazine, Issue 113,
                          October 2017

Sunk   Two Cities Review, Issue 12, Winter
                          2016

Piece of History   Fifth Wednesday Journal, Fall 2012,
                          Issue 11

Woodbine & Asters   Prairie Schooner, Vol. 80, No. 2
                          Summer 2006

Location! Location!   Hobart, #10, Summer 2009

For the Birds   High Shelf Press, XXXIII, August 2021

Aquatic Ape   GaiaLit, Issue No. 1, Spring/Summer
                          2021, Excerpted from the novel *Float*,
                          2013, Ashland Creek Press

Live Magical Moments   Quiddity, Vol. 4, No. 1, Spring 2011

When You Are Done   Sonora Review, No. 64/65, Spring 2014
Being Happy

As always, my deepest gratitude to the Raymond Street Writers Group, my first and best readers.

JOEANN HART's most recent book is the crime memoir *Stamford '76: A True Story of Murder, Corruption, Race, and Feminism in the 1970s.* Her novels are *Float*, a dark comedy about plastics in the ocean, and *Addled*, a social satire. *Arroyo Circle* is forthcoming from Green Writers Press in 2024. Her short fiction and essays have appeared in a wide range of literary publications, including Slate.com, Orion, The Hopper, Prairie Schooner, The Sonora Review, Terrain.org, and many others. *Highwire Act & Other Tales of Survival* is her first story collection.